The Chronicles of Arokah

Khali and the Orb of Xona

Mark Stibbe & Steve Brazier

Sarah GRACE PUBLISHING

Copyright © 2020 HexCel Designs Limited

23 22 21 20   7 6 5 4 3 2 1

First published 2020 by Sarah Grace Publishing
an imprint of Malcolm Down Publishing Ltd.
www.malcolmdown.co.uk

British Library Cataloguing in Publication Data
A catalogue record for this book is available from the British Library.

ISBN 978-1-912863-45-7 Hardback
ISBN 978-1-912863-49-5 Paperback

Illustrations by Sam Teale.
Cover design and artwork by Rebecca Anne Williams.
Art direction by Sarah Grace.
Additional design by Esther Kotecha.

Printed in Great Britain by Bell and Bain Ltd, Glasgow

Khali and the Orb of Xona is the first of a series of stories inspired by the discovery of a naturally occurring phenomenon. A unique group of shapes formed within the structure of a hexagon, combine to create the most beautiful and extraordinary patterns and designs. Many of them resemble snowflake and flower-like patterns found in nature.

Mark Stibbe is the award-winning, bestselling author of over fifty books including, most recently, the Christmas novel *King of Hearts*. He ghostwrites and edits books as part of his BookLab business.

Steve Brazier is the inventor of the award-winning Arokah puzzle game, a 23-piece puzzle for all ages and abilities with multiple challenges that test your skill and endurance time and time again!

Contents

1
Take Me to Xona

My father disappeared just after my twelfth birthday, while the two of us were visiting our sister planet Xona. He had told me to stay inside his Space Ranger while he went to investigate a strange light that was pulsating and throbbing, changing colours, fading and then reappearing. It was coming from a cave not far from our vessel.

"I'll keep transmitting until I reach the light," he had said. "Whatever happens, Khali, don't follow me. If the Creeper returns, or if I don't come back in time, the autopilot is set to take you home."

He turned to me before he disappeared into the cargo bay at the centre of the Ranger. He gestured, signalling our own, unique goodbye, his teal eyes widening, shimmering, glistening.

I love that colour. His colour.

I wasn't to know that this would be the last time I would ever see his face, although the neurons in what Dad used to call my "gut brain" were telling me that something was wrong.

At that time, Dad was the chief science officer of our home planet, Kel. Six months before, he had discovered an opening in the protective membrane around the upper atmosphere of Xona. He had spotted this because dust clouds from Xona had travelled upwards from the planet surface, passing through the hole, heading towards our own world. Dad had gone to investigate and found the opening, travelled through it, and then begun explorations to Xona. No one in our history had ever navigated beyond this membrane before - until Dad did, that is.

In the days and weeks that followed, Dad often journeyed to Xona. He refrained from landing on the planet because he observed that the entire surface was covered in a dense and dangerous-looking weed. I called this "The Creeper." It appeared when the sun rose, then retreated into the rocky terrain at dusk. Dad and I were almost the only ones that knew about this appearing and disappearing weed. It was our secret.

Every morning, the Creeper would appear. When the sun came out, tendrils would emerge from the organic weed, reaching upwards. These looked like long and slender, leafless organs – "appendages" my father called them. They stretched out towards other objects, seeking to wrap themselves around anything within their grasp, even other tendrils. To my mind, they resembled the ringlets of my father's black hair, except they were climbing not falling, twining not hanging.

The greatest marvel of all was what happened as the sun began to flood these spiralling tendrils. As the light bathed them, they transformed from the bland mass of the Creeper into luxurious flowers, plants and trees. Although no one on our planet knew the details about the Creeper, everyone had seen this display of life and colour. Dad had recorded images, edited them, and then broadcast them. From the start, this spectacle bedazzled us. A lot of our own planet is covered in volcanoes, red sand and grey rocks. We also have many lakes that provide us with water as well as a giant lake of fire which is spectacular. When we saw Xona's lush vegetation, it stopped us in our tracks. Some of the plants were as tall as trees and as green as emeralds.

During those months, Dad would return from his expeditions and share with me at bedtime what he had discovered that day. There were only the two of us now, and I had already set my heart on following in my father's footsteps, so I was a keen listener.

"It appears there are no people or creatures there, just plants," my father told me one bedtime, as our orange sun set.

"Why?"

"The atmosphere is unbreathable. Even though water is present, and it appears there are other similarities to our own planet, its composition is extremely unusual. We're not sure it could support independent life. We've searched extensively and seen no evidence."

My father paused before continuing. "But there's something else there, Khali. Something… well, an energy, a lifeforce, something that we've never seen or felt on Kel. I have given it a name. Arokah."

"What's Arokah?"

"Another time."

Each night, I pressed for more.

Then, one night, he told me.

"A few weeks ago, I went just beyond the opening in the upper atmosphere and hovered the other side. I was with Danguari, another scientist, one of the few people I trust. He understands how important it is to protect Xona's secrets, not to let them fall into the wrong hands, the hands of those who would use the planet's resources for their own ends."

Dad took a sip from a cup of water before he continued.

"Our planet is dying, Khali. And some who know this would stop at nothing to save it, including stealing everything that Xona has, with no regard for life on that planet, however different from ours."

"So, what did you do on Xona?" I asked.

"I left the Space Ranger and took some samples from the underside of the crust and then we came home. When we examined them the next day, it became clear that the atmospheric crust was made of a crystalized substance, and that this was composed of spores from the tendrils on the planet surface. It was as I was discovering this that there was an accident."

I gasped.

"Someone dropped one of the samples. A tiny cloud appeared and, before I had time to react, I had inhaled some of it. The effect was immediate. I felt my energy levels increase. My sense of perception became crystal clear. It was as if I could lift a great rock and understand the mysteries of the universe. The Arokah did this, Khali. It's extraordinary."

"How do you know it's safe?" I asked. "Maybe it's like radiation poisoning."

"We've conducted tests. The results are conclusive." Dad disentangled some of the curls in his hair before he continued. "It's so safe that Danguari and I have added a chamber in the Space Academy. It's designed for children who find learning difficult, children who become easily anxious. The effects have already been remarkable, both on their levels of calm and concentration."

Dad looked up towards the ceiling.

"There has been another effect on me personally," he said. "I dream more. Not just more frequently, but more deeply. About things from the past to do with Mum. Things in the future to do with you. Sometimes, the dreams about you, Khali, they are so precise and so clear that I believe they might even be prophetic."

"What have you seen?" I asked.

"So many questions," Dad replied. He sat up, gave me a kiss on my head, and went to the door. "So many questions," he repeated.

Then he smiled, switched out the light and left me in the darkness, my bedsheet tucked tightly around me, wide awake and wondering.

Four days later, after Dad had cooked our evening meal, he told me to have a shower, climb into bed then read my book until he came to tell me something new about Xona.

"I discovered something else today," he said a little while later, after reading me a story. He waited for me to ask him what it was. He smiled, knowing that I couldn't contain my curiosity.

I nudged him hard in the ribs.

He laughed before answering. "I found out what caused the hole in the membrane in the upper atmosphere of Xona."

I kicked him this time, then leaned my head on his chest. I could hear his heart beating faster as he spoke.

"You remember I told you about the volcanoes on Xona, that some of them are ten times the size of our own?"

I nodded.

"And that when they erupt, they send a single blast of energy upwards, like a cannon?"

I nodded again.

"Well, one of the largest must have erupted about seven months ago, because the ash blistered the underside of the crystalized crust in the upper atmosphere. That was what formed the hole that is allowing us to go and explore Xona."

I could barely contain my excitement.

"And there's more," he said. "You remember the trees and the flowers of Xona, that reach for the sun?"

I nodded.

"Their spores have permeated two science vessels that I set up as sentinels at the opening. Those on board have been experiencing increased strength and perception just as I have. Even a small exposure has a significant effect, higher doses a quite dramatic effect."

I looked up, turned, then stared into my father's face. Everything about him seemed to look different. Like the fact that his hair, which had turned white after my mother's death, had turned jet black again in recent weeks. Like the fact that his eyes had changed too. They had turned the colour of marble after our great sadness, but now they were a teal colour, like the oceans and great lakes in the southern hemisphere. Dad was alive again.

From that time on, the bedtime routine was my favourite time of the day. Every night, Dad would tell me more, and it seemed the more time he spent the far side of the membrane, the more he was energised by what he had found and mesmerised by what he had not.

"You'll like this," Dad said a few nights later.

"What? What? What?" I cried, repeating myself when his answer didn't come as quickly as I wanted.

Dad laughed. "You know how you love going fast on the hover bike I gave you?"

I nodded.

"Well, I have engineered some of the crystals from the membrane and created a jump drive for my Space Ranger." Then he added, "It goes unimaginably fast."

"No way!"

"It's true," my father insisted. "It's been taking me three days to get to Xona and three days to get back using my engines, but now I can do it in three hours using the jump drive."

I was so excited I didn't know what to say for several seconds. Until suddenly, I knew exactly what to say. "I want to see! Take me to Xona. Please, Dad. Please!"

Dad smiled, kissed me goodnight, and left my room, saying nothing.

The next night, as Dad rested on my bed in the darkness, I tried again. "Take me to Xona. Please, Dad."

"No, my son. You can see it here, from a safe distance."

"It's not the same," I said.

My father knew this in his heart. He knew that the nearer a person travelled to the surface of Xona, the more they would be revitalised. I wanted to experience that myself, although I didn't realise at the time that I had already begun to experience it, simply by being so close to my father.

After the fourth or fifth time of asking, Dad changed his reply. He sighed and asked, "What would your mother have said?"

I didn't tell him, but she would have said the same words she uttered before the sickness finally took her. I had overheard her as I stood outside the doorway to her cubicle in the hospital.

"Look after him, my darling. And look after yourself."

And then a long, drawn out groan.

Followed by the sound of my father crying.

That was the day of our great sadness.

That was the day our world seemed to end.

Until now. Now we were both captivated. This new fascination had taken a hold of us both, as if the Creeper on the surface of Xona had reached out and entwined itself around our hearts, pulling us with a force greater than loss towards its mysteries.

Exactly one week later, I woke on my twelfth birthday to find Dad standing next to my bed, carrying an object under his arm wrapped in silver paper. It was the size of my favourite picture of my family, hanging on the wall of my bedroom. "Happy birthday, my son," he said.

He lowered the gift on the floor while I clambered out of bed, beside myself with excitement. The object was a rectangular shape. It looked heavy. Really heavy.

I removed the paper. The rectangle was composed of two layers. The upper layer, covering the surface, was a sheet of Lagentum, a rare material that Dad had been given by his own father. The lower layer, a kind of base for the Lagentum sheet, was made of Drona Stone, mined from the hills surrounding the seas of basalt near the Dhavi Basin. This stone is the heaviest and densest material on our planet. I couldn't believe how easily Dad was carrying it.

"It's a puzzle," Dad said.

Intrigued, I knelt in front of the stone, which was now resting on its base. It was covered by unusual symbols. Each symbol looked like a letter, or a part of a letter, but I wasn't sure they were letters at all - not letters I could read anyhow. Each symbol was surrounded by a shape. As I started to sweep my hand over the surface of the Lagentum plaque on the front of the stone, the shapes began to move. There were 23 shapes altogether, each encompassing a mysterious symbol. As I played, I found I could create various patterns by moving different shapes around.

"This is very cool, Dad," I said, breathing fast. "But what exactly do I have to do?"

My father replied, "If you look carefully, you will see a flower-like pattern on the surface of the stone made up of seven sections. The challenge is to move each of the 23 pieces into those sections until they all lock into place. Once you do that, there is a surprise."

As I passed my hand over the plaque, every piece of the puzzle moved its position without me touching it, until I raised my hand from the tablet, when the shapes seemed to dock like ships in new positions, creating an entirely new arrangement of the same shapes and letters.

"What's the surprise?"

"If I told you, it wouldn't be a surprise now, would it?" Dad laughed. "You'll see when you've solved it."

"But that's not fair!" I said. "I have to go to school today. There's no way I can do this by tonight."

"Who said anything about tonight?"

I knew that it would have been impossible to do it that quickly. I had already begun the calculations. There were tens of thousands of variations, maybe even hundreds of thousands. Solving the puzzle would probably involve writing a programme and then letting it run for days and days and would, in the end, probably burn out my computer.

My father laughed. The black freckles on his dark-skinned cheeks seemed to jump as he did. "This could take you a while to solve," he said.

"I'll do it," I boasted.

That day I was restless at school, shutting down even more than usual, avoiding interactions with other students, absorbed in my thoughts. I had, and still have, a condition called Rhuba which means that I can understand the most complex equations, riddles, and puzzles, and yet I seem to be unable to master how to relate well to others. One in five people have it on our planet. That's ten million, five hundred, twenty-seven thousand, nine hundred and thirty-three people. That said, not everyone else has my form of Rhuba. We are all different. We are all unique. Everyone is special.

In the evening, when Dad came home from the Space Academy, I had already been working on the puzzle for several hours, moving the pieces this way and that, trying to lock them into their correct positions. We were sitting at the dining table and I was eating my birthday meal. He had made sure to keep the three ingredients from touching each other when he served them on my plate. They were like three separated islands on a silvery sea.

"It's really difficult, that puzzle," I cried. "Did you invent it?"

He nodded.

"Where did you get the idea from?"

"I've been having dreams. A lot of dreams. Particularly about this tablet. The shapes. The letters, everything."

"But how come the pieces move without me touching them?" I asked.

"Telekinetic focus," he replied. Then he added, "It's a very special gift for a very special child."

Dad made some hand signals and mouthed some words after he had said that. This was our secret sign. He pointed to his heart. Then turned the same hand upwards, raising two fingers. Then pointed to my heart.

I repeated the same actions.

Me to you.

You to me.

Then we both placed the same hand on our forehead before lifting it to the stars in the night sky.

Forever.

Dad took a deep breath and looked out of the window of my bedroom, out across the skyline of the city, towards the flame-red sun setting above the volcanic Mountains of Drebar. "I wish your mother had been here to see you on your birthday," he said.

I thought of Mum. I imagined her coming in with Dad and the stone tablet that morning, her white-skinned face lit up by her hazel eyes. Her smile, her laugh, the smell of her wavy brown hair when she hugged me. The hair that had disappeared when her treatments began. Along with her bright eyes and her even brighter smile.

"I miss Mum," I said.

Dad said nothing. He simply reached out a hand and clutched my shoulder, and I could tell by the tremor in his fingers that he still missed her too. Deeply.

"I've decided," he said when he pulled away.

"What, Dad?"

"We're going to Xona. Tonight! Let's call it a birthday treat."

I was the one trembling now.

"It will have to be another one of our secrets. I can arrange things so that we can leave without arousing any suspicion. It will take a bit of skill, but it's one of the advantages of being the boss that you know how to manage the security protocols. All the same, we will need to be very careful. You know the severe penalty for unauthorised flights."

I did. A week before it had been all over the news. A young space trooper had stolen one of our fighters and flown through the hole in Xona's upper atmosphere. He had somehow heard of what had happened to the scientists in the two sentinel ships and had been intent on pillaging some of the minerals from the underside of the crust. He had been caught and was waiting for his sentence. Everyone expected him to be sent to the Krobar jail.

"Be ready in an hour," Dad said, turning to leave the room.

I couldn't believe it.

So many of my pleas had fallen on deaf ears, or so I had thought.

Now I was going to Xona!

The Ranger was the latest version, a two-person runabout used primarily for scientific exploration

2
The Day I Froze

One hour later, Dad and I climbed onto our hover scooters and made our way down the side streets and alleyways of our great city, using the shadows for cover until we arrived at the space dock. We entered without raising any alarms, then hurried from his office down an unguarded passageway to Dad's sleek white Space Ranger. I had never been this close to it before. He had only shown me pictures.

The Ranger was the latest version, a two-person runabout used primarily for scientific exploration, with a cargo bay and bunks in the central section, impulse engines at the rear and clear windows made of transparent aluminium. The Ranger had my mother's name emblazoned in gold letters on each side of the oval-shaped cockpit window.

Doxana.

Half an hour later, Dad had done all he needed to alter the logs and cover our tracks. This was made easier because the sentinels on duty during the night were androids. Dad knew all the passwords and security codes, so it wasn't long before he had enabled us to leave undetected.

When Dad had performed the systems check, he powered up the engines and we left for Xona, skirting round a shower of phosphorescent meteors before he said, "Are you ready to experience the jump drive, Khali?"

I nodded, too excited to speak.

Dad pushed the white lever in front of him, grasping its silver handle with his right hand, thrusting it towards the console. As soon as it locked, I heard the crystalized energy beginning to grow in volume and power. After two seconds, it reached its summit and then thrust us into the dark space in front of us. It felt like we were in a kind of gigantic slipstream, and every object was momentarily blurred and extended, as if I was looking through the lens of a huge camera that was out of focus.

"This is crazy fun!" I cried.

Dad smiled. "You can play with the puzzle," he said. "It'll be nearly three hours before we arrive."

I loosened my straps and stepped back into the cargo bay. Sitting down on the floor next to the tablet, I began to draw my hand over the shapes, moving them this way and this, trying to achieve a design, an order, a symmetry from the dancing letters.

In what seemed no time at all, I heard Dad's voice. "I've switched off the jump drive."

We had reached the membrane. I sat in the co-pilot's seat in the cockpit and stared out of the front window.

"Look," Dad said, pointing through the rounded window to the layer around Xona's upper atmosphere. It shimmered with a blue-green colour, like his eyes, which were now full of longing.

I knew what that longing was all about. He had almost told me as much. Dad wanted to fill Kel with all the benefits of Arokah, so that everything, from our material structures to our physical tissues, would be rejuvenated by its life and health. He wanted to harness the energy of Arokah to improve our technology. But above all, he wanted to make sure no one would ever have to go through what we had suffered with my mother.

That was my longing too.

We passed through the vast opening and then through the centre of a cloud of dust from Xona.

"Do you see that?" Dad asked. "It's making its way out of the hole towards Kel. Some of our people have already spotted parts of our planet where the spores have alighted. They are already collecting and using the spores. We cannot stop it."

"Why is that so bad?" I asked.

"It's not bad," he said. "It will only become bad if bad people decide to abuse the spores. There need to be some protocols to prevent that, otherwise both our planets will suffer."

After that, there was silence, during which I tried to imagine how anyone would ever want to harm Xona. From time immemorial, our ancestors had called it The Great Sister. It felt like a part of us, connected, related, bound together like indivisible twins. It was beautiful, too; from Kel's vantage point, Xona looked like a giant, glistening moon, glowing with white and blue-green colours – "teal" my father called it. Passing through the opening, I now realised why. What we were now observing was the crystalized crust around the planet and it was this shimmering, teal membrane that our people had always seen. No, I couldn't understand how any person on our planet would ever want to do anything other than respect and honour Xona.

Dad broke the silence. "Ok, we're starting our descent." Some minutes later, at a safe distance from Xona, Dad reset the thrusters and the Doxana came to a halt, hovering above the surface of the planet.

"Let's have a look," he said.

He placed a visor over my eyes and patched the optics into the cameras in the belly of the Ranger. Within seconds, we both saw it. The Creeper was sprawling across the planet and glowing in the dying sunlight. Its thick tendrils were moving slowly this way and that. It was even creepier this close to the surface. The images back home had not done it justice.

"Look at these!" Dad said.

Dad had trained the Doxana's cameras on a part of the planet's surface where the sun was shining more brightly. At first, all I could make out was a mess of colours, like the paints on my palette at school. But then, as my eyes focused, I saw what Dad had tried to describe to me during my many bedtimes. Flowers of a thousand different colours and forms. Trees of every shape. Plants of every description. Some were as tall as a mountain and as wide as a lake, others as short and thin as me. A multitude of different mainly pastel colours, different fronds, different shades and different fruits, an endless, multicoloured forest of life. Life tinged with teal.

"It's amazing, Dad!"

"I know," he said. "It's one thing seeing faraway images on your screen. It's another thing seeing it this near, this clear."

He was right. Like the difference between remembering my father's face and seeing it, up close and personal.

"Now look at this."

I gazed at a flower on which Dad had trained the cameras. He told me to look past the pale blue and already-fading yellow petals, the anthers and filaments, right into the white heart of the plant.

"What do you see?"

"It's a hexagon!" I cried.

"That's right. They are everywhere. Not just in the flowers either. They seem to be embedded in the rock, millions upon millions of hexagons, millions and millions of years old."

The light was beginning to fade now, and the trees were descending into the rocky surface of the planet.

"They come out when the sun rises," Dad remarked.

"And disappear at dusk," I added.

"My little professor!" Dad said, using his and Mum's favourite nickname for me.

Just then, something began to change. The flowers and trees all disappeared, leaving only the Creeper on the surface. But the Creeper was adapting, morphing. Instead of a great tangle of weed, it had now shifted from chaos to order, from shapelessness to symmetry.

"That's strange," Dad muttered. "I haven't seen it do this before."

As we both observed the Creeper, its entire mass began to shift creating a square shaped space. Below it, what looked like a very flat and rocky surface emerged. Its epicentre resembled a landing zone.

"I need to get closer," Dad said.

"Are you sure?" I asked.

"We must," he answered. "There's something down there drawing us. It's so powerful. Do you not feel it, Khali?"

I couldn't argue with that as Dad powered the thrusters, turning the nose of the Ranger toward the gap formed by the parting Creeper.

"There," he said, pointing to the space that looked flat and wide enough to land.

Forty seconds later we had landed, and Dad was already in the cargo bay, taking samples of the soil and the weed, testing the unfiltered spores from the edges of the Creeper. "It's way more potent than the spores on the underside of the membrane," he cried. "This is beyond anything we've tested so far."

It was just then that I felt it. A judder at the rear of the Ranger. A shaking of the entire vessel, first left, then right, while the bulkheads groaned.

"Damn it!" Dad shouted.

I had never heard him swear before. "What's the matter?" I cried.

"One of the tendrils," he answered. "I think it's wrapped itself around our engines. I'm going to have to go and have a look."

Dad was already reaching for his spacesuit in the cargo bay before I had a chance to tell him to be careful. I could see it all playing out on the monitor in front of me on the console in the cockpit.

Dad stepped out of the craft and onto the planet just as the sun went down, and the light with it.

"I'll switch on the lights," he said, his voice crackling through the speakers in the Ranger.

Light poured out of the front, sides, back and belly of the Ranger, illuminating everything within the range of my vision. The Creeper, which had been close enough to the Ranger, began to twist and turn.

Dad dimmed the lights until they were barely on at all. Then I watched as the mass of tentacles around the craft seemed to move as one, retreating into the ground, embedding themselves in the dense material of the planet as if the rocks were its home.

"The weed has let go," Dad said. "We're free to leave. I'm coming back on board."

Then it happened. Dad was about to reenter the cargo bay when something caught his eye, then mine. It was coming from a small opening in a volcanic mountain.

A light.

Tiny at first.

Then growing.

On and off.

Short bursts.

Long bursts.

First one colour, then another colour.

"Looks like a signal," Dad said.

I saw on the monitor that he was walking from the stern to the conical bow of the Ranger as he was speaking.

When he arrived, he stood in front of the Doxana, his hands on his hips, staring through the glass bubble of his helmet out into the dark and towards the light. "I'm going to have to take a look," he said.

"Please don't, Dad," I said, feeling the onset of a nausea in the pit of my stomach. "You can send Dangauri next time."

But I knew, even before Dad responded, that time was the problem. As we had approached the membrane earlier, Dad had told me something that had been worrying him, something he hadn't yet told the other members of the Space Academy on Kel.

"The opening I discovered. It's slowly closing. I don't know why it's happening or how, but it seems that the gap is resealing itself. Maybe it's the healing properties of the spores, but at the current speed, we have about a month or so left for excursions to Xona. It may be centuries until the next big volcano erupts and an opening occurs."

Outside the Ranger, Dad turned towards me so that I could see his face in the one dim light still pouring from the Ranger.

"No," I said. "Please, Dad. I don't like it."

"You'll be all right," he said. "If anything happens, I've set the autopilot to get you home. When you get back to Kel, leave the Ranger when it docks. Go straight home and tell no one what you've done or what you've seen. I've made sure that no one will ever know you were here."

"It's not me I'm worried about," I said, my voice now raised. "It's you, Dad."

"Don't worry, Khali," he said. "I'll keep in constant communication with you. I've got three hours of oxygen. Should be more than enough. Just wait here and be ready to respond whenever I call. Don't record what I say on the Ranger's systems. Use the communications pad I've left for you. It's in the overhead compartment just above you."

I stood, opened the panel, and retrieved a white framed pad. I took it and held it in both hands. My father's voice now came through the small speaker on its front. A flickering red light told me that our conversations were being recorded on the device.

As my father turned again towards the light, my mother's last words poured out of my mouth before I had even had time to think. "Look after yourself, Dad."

The teal light in his eyes dimmed. "I promise," he said. Then he lifted his hand and mouthed a silent goodbye.

Me to you.

You to me.

Forever.

I did the same.

And my heart sank like the sun.

My father walked off into the darkness. For the next hour, there were very few transmissions, just routine descriptions of the soil and the rocks. Then the comms came faster.

"I'm at the mouth of the cavern. Khali, it's enormous, the size of a mountain. I'm going in…"

Silence for 119 seconds.

"I'm inside, going down some steps. The walls … There are letters everywhere. It's like a strange language."

Silence again.

Three minutes and six seconds this time.

"I'm in a tunnel … following the light … leaving markers." Five more minutes, and 37 seconds.

"Coming to the end. Big lake … clear as crystal."

Silence again.

Ten minutes and 45 seconds this time.

I was counting.

I had worked out every minute, every second, in my head.

"You have to come back now, Dad!" I shouted. "You haven't enough oxygen!"

No answer.

Then, after nearly fifteen minutes, "There's a light here, Khali … As big as the cave. Enormous."

I felt a rising sense of panic. I started to practice the calming strategies my mother had taught me, pressing the palm of my left hand with the index finger of my right hand. Pressing so hard, in fact, that my fingernail broke the skin, producing red lines.

I changed my breathing too, trying to give my body a break from the anxiety that would otherwise have engulfed me.

Then there was another crackle.

"Remember these numbers," Dad said.

He read out a series of numbers, and for the duration of two readings, the signal was strong. I spent the next few minutes repeating them until I knew they were stored in my memory.

Then there were three more transmissions.

"There's some sort of hive mind, like our bees. Everything connected … nothing random … right across the planet."

Crackle.

"I love you, my son. Always."

Then the last one.

"Takes your breath away."

Silence.

Like the deathly quiet after the sound of the flatline from the monitor next to my mother's hospital bed.

As my panic grew, my eyes turned to the stone puzzle nearby. I hadn't thought of it while Dad was away in the cave, but now I stood and imagined I was the tablet. I drew my hands to my chest, as if I was wearing a breastplate of Lagentum, as if my heart was covered in the strange letters, or parts of letters, embedded in each of the 23 shapes. Until I and the stone were one.

Cold.

Inanimate.

Impermeable to pain.

I froze so effectively that I was unaware of the chirruping of the console or the murmur of the thrusters.

As the Ranger rose towards the hole in the membrane, back towards Kel, I remained in my self-imposed, cryogenic state, until the alarm in the cockpit awakened me, telling that the Ranger had docked and that it was time for me to head back to the apartment.

I left the space dock on my own kind of autopilot, heading for the doors out of the facility. The sun was beginning to rise. It wouldn't be long before the workers arrived.

As I stepped onto my hover scooter and switched on the engine, it hit me.

Dad was gone.

He wasn't coming back. I was on my own now.

3
You Can Call Me Matron

Once home, I sat on my bed and cried as the sun rose and the city outside my bedroom window burst into life. When my sobbing stopped, I noticed that my left hand was hurting. I opened my palm and saw the dried blood where my fingernail had broken the surface of my skin just four hours before. As I looked more closely, I saw that I had imprinted six connected lines in a six-sided shape. A blood red hexagon! I was shocked. Every time I had used this calming strategy in the past, I had drawn four lines, the shape of a square, and I had never drawn blood. The whole exercise was supposed to be like a finger massage. But not last night. Not on the Doxana.

I was feeling tired and emotional, and fast too, as if I was still moving through space at the lightning speed of the jump drive. Since my hand was hurting, I decided to calm myself with Mum's breathing exercise. This involved breathing in for four seconds, then breathing out for four seconds, then breathing in for four seconds, then breathing out, again for four seconds. The whole thing was supposed to be in two lots of fours, in and out, in and out. In my head, the shape of a square. Square breathing.

Only it wasn't.

For some reason, I did *three* lots of in and out, not two.

And I counted for six seconds each time, not four. This was a new exercise. Hexagonal, not square. And strangely, it seemed to work. *Mum would be proud of me*, I thought.

I owed so much to my mum for helping me deal with my condition. Eight years before, she had been the one who first noticed my inability to play with other children while I was at nursery school. When the other boys and girls were happily talking to each other and the teachers, I was withdrawn from the very beginning, focused intensely on small objects, like lonely bricks and puzzle pieces. One time there was a fire drill at nursery school, and I was so fixated on a problem-solving board that a teacher raised her voice at me for not getting up and joining the march to safety outside. My response? I froze to the spot, unable to cope with the volume of her voice. I was simply not used to it; Mum never shouted.

My teacher talked to my mother about it, and it was then that Mum started to suspect that I had the neurological disorder called Rhuba. I was two years old and she took me for tests. The medical officer confirmed her diagnosis and from then on people just accepted the unusual way my mind worked. Everyone chose to see it as a different ability, not a disability.

One time, I was trying to help my parents after a meal and was carrying my dirty plate towards the silver basin.

"Just throw it in the sink," Dad said.

I hurled the plate into the basin, smashing it into thirty-seven pieces. From then on, seeing my distress at their reaction, Mum and Dad avoided using words that I would take literally.

Another time, I was at school and my language teacher was instructing us about idioms. One of the phrases confused me. He talked about the common saying that a person is "made of money".

I couldn't grasp for the life of me how an inhabitant of Kel could be constructed of the same metal we use for our planet's currency. For the rest of the lesson, I was desperately trying to work out how this could be.

I carried this puzzle into my next lesson, which was Maths. Halfway through an exercise at our desks, I took some ancient coins from a display on my left and lay on the floor. While the teacher at the front was marking, his attention distracted, I covered my thighs and chest with the coins.

"Look!" I cried when I had finished. "I'm made of money!"

No one giggled because on our planet such a reaction can be interpreted as "laughing at" someone. On Kel, children and adults whose minds work differently are regarded as unique. We are honoured, not stigmatised or pitied. And this applies to all those with Rhuba, not just those who have a special talent. *Dreamers*, as they're called. This is one of the most beautiful things about my home world. I have always loved the way the Ahketans, our rulers, have created a culture where people who seem different are not excluded. And that's why, once my Rhuba was recognised, I was never bullied, nor told off by teachers for not being able to do something alien to the way my mind worked. They simply gave me a task on which I could give my full attention, knowing that this would sometimes lead to amazing results.

And that's really the point. It's the reason why the Ahketans had learned, over many centuries, not to isolate those whose minds were able to focus – hyper-focus, in fact – on details that others completely missed. Many of our greatest inventors, engineers, scientists, artists and pioneers have been diagnosed with Rhuba. They are champions.

I tell you all this because I am about to share with you what happened after my father's disappearance on Xona, and I don't want you to think for a moment that the way I share the story means I don't care. I did. And I still do. It's just that when I talk about things that are upsetting, I'm not good with my feelings. Sometimes I can get over-upset. Sometimes I can seem cut off, almost uncaring. It's just the way I am.

So, then, here's what I know.

When I left the Ranger on my return to Kel, it returned to land on Xona just as the sun was coming out and was crushed into tiny fragments by the Creeper. A probe later that same morning followed the flight path of the Doxana and its analysts deduced that my father had been killed in a terrible accident. They didn't know that Dad had gone to the cave to look at the light, nor that he had given those numbers to me.

Also, no one knew that I had gone straight home with the tablet on my hover scooter, undetected, to our apartment overlooking the city. That I had got ready for school. Studied hard throughout the day. Returned home, knowing that Dad was gone, that I was alone, at least for a few seconds. For, no sooner had I entered my home when a man and a woman appeared. I could see from the security screen inside the front door that they were in Space Academy uniforms. That they were high-ranking officers, with four gleaming silver buttons on the woman's blood red epaulettes. Three on his.

"We're friends of your father," the man said.

"May we see you, Khali?" the other one asked.

I pressed the button to let them in.

When they arrived, they asked me to sit down. The woman sat close to me on our sofa. I asked her to go and sit on the chair opposite. I didn't like people invading my personal space.

I didn't like looking into strangers' eyes, either. When one of them spoke to me, I turned my attention to the person who wasn't speaking.

"Your father," the woman said, struggling with her words. I looked at the man. He had a moustache with some specks of food – it looked like *guana* - in the right-hand corner. "He's missing, most probably dead."

I nodded.

"He left instructions if anything like this was ever to happen…"

"Yes," the man interrupted. "Given your circumstances…"

I now looked at his colleague. She had a dark brown mole on her left cheek, with three tiny hairs. "He means the death of both your parents," the woman interjected.

I nodded again. "I'm an orphan," I said, looking away from them. "That's okay. It can't be helped. It is what it is."

The woman seemed to me to be concerned at this and turned to her companion. "You tell him," she said.

The man took out a pad and began to read. "Your father's last will states that this apartment is to be sold and the money – which will be considerable, given the location and the view – should fund your education. His desire is that you go to the Space Academy and study to become a science officer. He says that you show exceptional skills, particularly in mathematical and scientific topics, and that he anticipates that you will become a unique cadet, an alumnus of the Academy, far surpassing his own achievements."

I did not respond to this. I saw no reason to; I could already tell, from just one day at school, that I had been exposed to the spores on my visit to Xona. I knew that my sense of perception and my physical strength were increasing. Last night, I had managed to lift the heavy stone containing the puzzle as if it was no lighter than a feather.

"There is a residential centre at the Space Academy," the woman said. "It's called the Beacon and it's where the Academy students who have no parents are accommodated. You'll board there until you're 18, when you will graduate if you work hard."

"I won't be 18," I muttered.

"Pardon?" the woman said.

"I'll be far younger than that."

"I'm afraid you're only allowed a few belongings," the man said. "You'll have your own quarters, but they are very small, certainly not as spacious as this apartment."

I had already decided what I'd take. Some things belonging to my mother, that I had kept in my closet, in her bag with the floral design. The white communication device from the Doxana, and my father's silver-rimmed pad, which I had hidden before they arrived, because I knew they would ask for it, which they did. A few clothes, including my father's ceremonial uniform. A photograph in which my parents are standing behind me, arm in arm. Mum is kissing Dad. I am looking at the camera, talking to the photographer about his equipment, telling him what each item is called, the model, the functionality, the price. All this with a deadpan face, while my parents laugh and the cameraman smiles. And finally, my father's present, the puzzle.

"You have an hour before you're picked up," the man concluded.

As the automatic door slid open, the woman turned to me. "I'm so sorry that you've lost your father," she said.

I looked away and frowned. "I didn't lose him," I said, stomping with my words.

"What do you mean?"

"He got lost all on his own," I replied.

With that, she and her colleague left. I, meanwhile, found and folded some clothes and placed most of them in my bag, along with my mother's smaller flower-covered bag, the photograph, and the two electronic devices. The puzzle I covered and concealed in the folds of Dad's uniform.

Fifty-six minutes later, the shuttle arrived.

"You're four minutes early," I said to the pilot.

"I am," she replied. The person in the pilot's uniform was young. Maybe eighteen. Dyed grey hair. Short at the sides. Wavy and thicker on top. Very cool. Obviously spent time on it. Black eyebrows to offset the grey. And a tattoo between the wrist and the elbow on the underside of the right arm. A skull, surrounded by roses, with the word MOTHER imprinted on the petals, one letter on each.

"What's your name?" I asked.

"Demorah." Her voice was deadpan.

Demorah turned around and gathered a zip-up suit carrier from the empty co-pilot's seat. "Put this on. It's your uniform. We have your personal data file, so your uniform was fitted today." Once again, her voice was far away and indifferent, almost robotic.

I stepped into the darker area at the rear of the vessel to change my clothes. I put on the white undershirt and the navy-blue trousers. I then dressed in the navy-blue jacket with its red epaulettes (no silver buttons). Finally, I looked at the insignia on my chest. The words "Space Academy" were stitched in white above a picture of the first rocket built and launched on Kel. It all felt quite tight, but I was happy with that. Tight clothes always calmed me. Like a hug from a mum or a dad.

I sat down at the back as the shuttle ascended, climbing vertically until it hovered over the thousands of high-rise buildings, their windows glowing with light in the pitch-black sky.

Twenty-three minutes later, we approached a gigantic, see-through dome, made of transparent aluminium, covering what looked to me like a small city. Buildings, so many buildings, some low level, others about halfway up the semi-sphere. And lights everywhere.

"It's amazing," I said, but Demorah didn't answer.

Our runabout docked in the shuttle port. Demorah helped me carry my belongings to a motorail station, then stood with me on the train as it sped from one side of the dome to the other, taking thirty-nine minutes, not including the time taken at each stop on the way.

I saw the Beacon before Demorah pointed it out. The tallest building in the area, rising into the darkness of the upper levels of the dome, an enormous tower with a lighthouse at its summit, shedding golden beams this way and that as its great bulb rotated.

By the time we arrived in the foyer, the students were all in bed, so we were met by a woman about 50 years old with a white uniform that had become a little too tight around her ginormous boobs. I thought they were going to burst from her zip-up blouse and leap out at me.

"Your name is Demorah, isn't it?" she said to the young pilot.

My companion nodded.

"Thank you," she said. "You've been most helpful."

Demorah looked at me before leaving and said, "I'll see you soon at our lessons at school."

Once we were alone, the woman said, "Khali?"

I nodded.

"Welcome to the Academy." She took my hand and led me down a corridor to a room with a single bed, a small desk with an odour-free plant on it, a chair, built-in cupboards and a shower cubicle in an adjoining room. The walls were painted in a powdery pale blue colour. The ceiling was painted a dark blue colour and had stars and planets on it.

"This is yours, darlink."

I would quickly learn that she never said "darling". I liked that.

"You can call me Matron," she added. Then her face became serious. "Have you eaten?"

I shook my head.

She led me down two corridors, painted in light pink, into the kitchens, where she located a robot. The machine was a catering droid designed and programmed to feed the 354 students at the Beacon. However, it had clearly been defaced. Someone had put a brown, wavy wig on the small sphere that passed for its head and drawn lipstick on the front of the face. To top it all, they had also hung two huge, plastic breasts on the rectangular metal body beneath, at the top of what looked like an oven door.

"Oh dear," Matron said. "One of our clever little darlinks has been defacing the chefbot again."

She opened a keypad at the back of its head.

"Turn away," she said.

I covered my eyes but left just enough of a gap between my fingers to see the numbers she was pressing. 7, 9, 6, 2. The machine flared into life, rising to twice its size.

"What do you want, darlink?" it asked. The voice, which came from the chefbot, seemed strange to my ears, more like Matron's than a droid's.

"Oh no!" Matron said. "They've been at it again."

She pressed some of the keys on a remote she had just produced from her utility belt.

6, 2, 1, 0.

I was looking without pretending not to now. Matron was far too focused on solving the problem to see what I was doing.

"Vocal activation," she said.

She pressed 1, 3, 7, 4.

"Restore default settings."

The droid spoke again, this time in a more mechanical monotone. "What do you require?"

Matron turned and asked me the same question.

"Sweet and sour noodles, and fizzy hot chocolate, please," I answered.

The droid moved to a work surface and issued a series of commands to three smaller droids, less spherical and rotund. Within seven seconds, the piping drink was in my hands, steam pouring from the top.

"Sit here," Matron said.

The drink was delicious, as were the noodles, which arrived thirty seconds later. By the time I had finished, I was beginning to feel tired. It had been a long day, and an even longer night before it, and I had exerted a lot of energy managing my distress.

"Time for bed," Matron said as she shut down the chefbot.

"Aren't you going to clean the chefbot up?" I asked, pointing to the wig and the fake boobs.

Matron paused, smiled, and then shrugged. "Let the little darlinks have their fun."

Three minutes later, we were back in my room.

"You unpack your clothes," Matron said, pressing a button on the wall, at which four invisible drawers opened from the white wall. "And put the clothes that need hanging up in the built-in wardrobe."

No buttons were needed to reveal the wardrobe. I could see the latticed door and the glass handle on the other side of the room.

"I'll be back in ten minutes," Matron said. "I've got a special surprise for you. I think you'll love it. But I'm only giving it to you if your clothes are unpacked, your room is tidy and you're ready for bed."

I was intrigued.

"I hope you like fluffy things," Matron said, looking back over her shoulder, as the door closed with a hiss.

"It's called a qark," Matron said, as the creature began to press down on my knees with its front paws. "All the newbies at the Beacon have one."

4
A Very Hairy Empath

Exactly nine minutes and 58 seconds later, Matron returned bearing something under her arm. It looked quite large to my eyes, although I couldn't work out what it was because Matron had covered it with a pillowcase the same dark blue colour and texture as my bedclothes. I thought I saw the object move and then twitch, but I couldn't be sure. It might have been a trick caused by the lighting.

"Here we are, darlink," Matron said, sitting down next to me on the edge of my small bed.

"What is it?"

"Before I show you, do you have any allergies, such as to animal hair, or reactions to certain colours?"

"Some primary colours hurt my eyes."

"Have you ever been bitten or harmed by a pet?"

"I was once stung by one of Dad's bees, but it was my fault. I got over it quickly and it turns out I was lucky. I wasn't allergic to the bee sting, like some other children are."

"How are you with animals?"

"I prefer them to people."

Matron smiled. "Then I think you two are going to get along just fine," she said.

She drew the pillowcase away and revealed a four-legged creature unlike anything I had ever seen. It was about the size of my pillow, when you included its masses of light grey, cloudy white, pale brown and teal hair, which had a strange sheen to it, like soft satin. On its head, the creature had a sweeping lilac mullet, which was matched evenly by the abundance of hair covering its tail. The hair on its body was plentiful too, so plentiful, in fact, that I couldn't tell whether the animal was fat or thin or somewhere between. As Matron placed the creature on my lap, its shaggy tail reached upwards and shuddered, as if shaking away a troublesome insect. I loved it immediately.

"It's called a qark," Matron said, as the creature began to press down on my knees with its front paws. "All the newbies at the Beacon have one."

The animal looked at me with its large black eyes, its wide and curving nose sniffing and snorting, its ten kinked whiskers vibrating. I, who found looking into a stranger's eyes a challenge, couldn't help returning the stare, mesmerised by the animal's gaze, which seemed to be looking not just at me, but through me too.

"What's a qark?"

"It's an empath, darlink. It discerns what you're feeling, and sometimes what others are feeling in the room, and then it tells anyone who's looking at it what that feeling is."

"How?"

"Through its tail, darlink, and through its eyes."

As soon as she had said the words, the tail rose up to its full height and started to tremble like an antenna.

"Is it feeling what I'm feeling?" I asked.

Matron nodded.

The qark's tail finished its shiver. Then its eyes began to change colour, from pitch black to orange.

"It transmits your mood through its eyes," Matron said.

"What does it mean?" I asked.

"All the colours can mean two things. One positive. One negative. You must learn to interpret which it is from the context. So, for example, orange can mean warm, like the sun rising, or exhausted, tired and sluggish, like you often feel when the sun goes down."

Sluggish was exactly how I felt.

"What's its name?" I asked as the creature slid in and out of my legs, rubbing itself against the fabric of my pyjamas.

"You decide."

"It seems to like my legs, so I'll call it Shin."

"That's a good name, darlink. That could be a girl or a boy's name, which is very appropriate."

"Why?"

"A qark doesn't have a gender," Matron said. "It chooses whether to be male or female, depending on what's most advantageous to it. So, right now, it's choosing to be male, because it senses that's what it needs to be for you. It's gender-variant."

The qark was now resting on my lap, its nose buried into the palm of my outstretched hand, nudging and sniffing me playfully. Its whiskers tickled my fingers and I laughed.

"Also," Matron said, "it's very adaptable."

She could see the confusion on my face.

"That means it changes, depending on the needs of the newbie. Some of our students are easily overwhelmed by a touch, taste, sound, sight or smell. The qark detects this and changes its colour, texture, noises, odour, and so on, to meet the needs of its keeper."

I stroked Shin's head, running my fingers through its forelock.

Matron withdrew a torch-pen from her belt and shone it onto a white patch on the wall. When she turned the torch off, the picture remained on the space above my bed. As I squinted, I saw that it was a colour chart, with two vertical columns, one with a plus sign above it, the other with a minus sign. Each vertical column was divided into rows with the name of a different colour for each.

I started reading.

	+	-
Red	Passionate, enthusiastic	Angry
Grey	Strong, steady, rocklike	Sad
Blue	Peaceful	Mysterious, crafty
Pink	Playful, fun	Babyish, immature
White	Kind, good	Cold

I was about to read on when Matron spoke again. "Time for lights out, sleepy eyes," she said. "When you're ready, just tell the lights to dim or go off. They're voice activated, like everything else. I'll wake you in the morning for breakfast."

"May I ask a question before you go?" I said.

"Of course, darlink."

"What does Shin eat?"

"Popcorn," she replied. "There are bags of it in a box at the bottom of your cupboard. Give him a bowl every morning when you get up and every night before you go to sleep."

Matron could see that I was about to ask another question and pre-empted me. "No need to tonight. Shin's already been fed."

With that, she passed through the automatic doors.

"Dim the lights," I said.

The cubicle descended into a warmer tone.

I sat and stroked Shin gently on his long, soft back. The more tired I became, the more the creature's eyes glowed with that deep orange colour I had noticed before.

Sleepy as I was, I decided not to climb into bed. Instead, I removed the tablet from my father's briefcase, standing it upright next to the empty wall space beside the door. I sat in front of it and stared at it while Shin circled me, purring and yawning, emitting a high-pitched squeak every time its jaws drew themselves out to their widest point. The squeal would descend as the jaws retracted into a satisfied grin.

I passed my hand over the Lagentum plate and started rearranging the shapes to form the coherent symmetry of the puzzle challenge. I still couldn't see a way forward, even though I thought in patterns all the time. The symbols also seemed so mysterious, other-worldly even, and I couldn't make sense of any of it. Not yet, anyhow.

I reached for my backpack and withdrew my father's silver communicator pad, which I had hidden. Perhaps there was something in its files, some keys or clues, to help me find the solution.

The pad powered up and the screen lit up with it, revealing a photograph of my mother in happier and healthier times, laughing on a holiday beside one of the Great Lakes of Lubar. Her eyes were shiny and alive. Her wavy hair as long and fulsome as Shin's.

I knew my father's password.

Doxana40.

My mother's name and age. Her age when she died, that is.

Straightaway, the image disappeared and was replaced by my father. Something had self-activated in his device and Dad was now staring at me, his warm eyes looking into the camera, his hand adjusting the angle of the picture so that his head and shoulders were fully visible. I could tell from the background that he was in his office at work. The orange sun was setting through the window behind his head.

"Hello Khali," he said, his voice soft and soothing. "If you're watching this, it's because I'm gone and I'm not coming back. I'm so sorry. I know you will be suffering."

His eyes were watery.

Mine were too.

As Shin came and lay over my feet, keeping them warm, my father continued. "I'm speculating that you're now at the Beacon, because that's what I have stipulated in my will. I hope you still have the stone puzzle, your birthday present, with you. It is vital that you keep hold of it, and that it doesn't fall into anyone else's hands."

As he said this, my father looked around him, as if there might have been something in the shadows watching him.

"Some of our people have discovered that the spores of Xona and the crystals in the membrane have immense power. You and I know that there's an energy generating the spores, the like of which we have never known on our planet. This energy, which you and I call Arokah, could save Kel in the future. But we must take great care. There are those on our home world who would use it for their own selfish ends."

My father looked behind him, then to his left and right, as if he was being watched. I could tell he was anxious not to be overheard. "Listen," he whispered. "I believe the Arokah is neither good nor bad. It's how it's used that is important."

Dad tipped the screen towards him for five seconds, as if someone had come into the room. He then restored it to its former position, his eyes staring into the camera again.

"In one of my experiments, I exposed the puzzle stone to the spores, Khali, so you will already be feeling the effects. You are my little professor and I know I can trust you. Use the power of Arokah wisely and well. Don't let it fall into the wrong hands."

Then he paused and smiled.

"I may be a little biased, but I think you are the most insightful and articulate boy on our planet. A child prodigy, a young genius, no less. These qualities are only going to increase the more you spend time within the energy field of Arokah."

My father frowned.

"But Arokah isn't all-powerful. For example, the spores do not seem to have the power to affect the Rhuboid brain. They can enhance our strength and perception, but they cannot change the way we think. Indeed, and this is a mystery to me, it's almost as if they do not want to."

Dad's voice was barely audible now as he leant close to the microphone on his pad. "I know you can guard the power of Arokah. I may not be there in body to see it, but I will be watching in spirit, looking at you as you grow up, cheering you on, my son."

A single tear fell down his face.

Then he started to signal.

Our familiar signal.

Me to you.

You to Me.

Forever.

Shin looked up from my feet.

His eyes were grey.

The colour of sadness.

The colour of determination.

I took Shin under my arm and sat on the edge of my bed, stroking the tufts of sweeping hair on his head. Just as I was about to turn in for the night, I heard the hiss of the door to my room.

There was a tall figure standing in the half light at the threshold.

Dark hair and stubble under a hood.

What looked like hovering crystals above his shoulders and forehead.

A long robe over a collarless shirt.

A thick black belt with golden studs.

Knee length, black leather boots, with golden buckles.

A golden medallion on his chest, hanging from a golden chain from his pitted neck, with an engraving of a lighthouse on its front, the emblem of the Beacon, my new home.

"Who are you?" I asked.

The man didn't answer. His eyes were staring at the tablet. The more he looked, the more his pupils seemed to grow larger.

"What is it?" he asked, turning towards me.

"A gift from my father," I replied.

I looked away from him, choosing instead to look at Shin, whose eyes had changed from orange to gold.

"I am sorry for your loss," the man said.

I nodded.

"I have a gift of my own to give you," he said.

I turned as he stretched out his right hand. My eyes were drawn as much to the scar from his wrist to his thumb as they were to the golden band in the rough-skinned palm.

"How did you get that?"

"Let's just say I had an argument with a predator," he said.

I nodded, trying to picture the scene in my head.

"Here," the man said, offering the gift. "It's the latest Time Keeper from the Hour Glass Corporation. It records all your experiences, your memories, your feelings, in a tiny microchip. It not only tells you the time, it also tells you about time. About how you've spent your time over the course of your life. Plug it into your personal work pad and it will offer you a single, coherent story out of all the fragments of your days."

He handed me the golden wrist band, containing four tiny and old-fashioned dials in each corner of the display, and a screen in a hexagonal shape in the middle.

"Thank you," I said, taking the band, which wrapped itself around my left wrist without me touching it.

The man smiled. "In answer to your question," he continued, "the students here call me the Guardian."

He looked back at the tablet. I could tell he was gazing at its patterns, its lettering, its mysteries.

"We should talk some more about your father's gift," he said, turning to go. "But for now, you must be exhausted, so get some rest."

The door hissed again.

I was left with a head that was sore from trying to work out what on Kel was going on.

There was only one thing for it.

Bed.

Shin's eyes were still pulsating with a golden colour as I climbed under my silver, heat-retaining blanket. I had just enough energy to study the colour chart above my bedhead as I found the most comfortable position. Before my command to dim the lights, I found the column I was looking for on the chart behind me.

Gold.

Plus means generous.

Minus means greedy.

I yawned as my eyelids grew heavy.

I stared up at the stars and planets on the ceiling, now glowing with a phosphorescent colour. As I pulled my dark blue covers tightly over and around me, I imagined my bed was a Space Ranger heading towards one of the planets on the ceiling, which seemed to be shining a little more brightly than the others. As I headed further up and further into the darkness of space, I descended deeper and deeper into the realm of sleep, my qark snuggling my feet.

5
Neurodiversity Rules!

That night, I had the first of my dreams about my father. They were mostly to follow the same pattern.

Me walking into a huge tunnel, which I guessed lay beyond the opening to the cave where my father disappeared.

Seeing a flickering light in the distance.

Passing through damp chambers and corridors, their walls covered in geometric symbols and hieroglyphs.

Arriving at the edge of a great lake.

The light in the distance growing stronger, coming nearer, crossing the lake from the darkness of the cavern to where I'm standing, at the edge of the water, which is dead calm.

Then, out of the light, my father appears, his arms beckoning me, calling out, begging me to come and bring him home.

I cry out, "DAD!" and run to him.

Only for the dream to end, and for me to wake up in a sweat, just before feeling his embrace.

That's what I dreamt my first night. Only when I awoke, I saw Matron standing next to my bed.

"Having a bad dream, darlink?"

I rubbed my eyes and looked away.

"What was it about?"

"Dad."

Matron rubbed her chin, then frowned. "Do you want to see the counsellor? She's a very good listener."

I shook my head.

"Well, you get dressed and join the line for breakfast in the corridor next to the kitchen. All meals are in silence. Some of the Rhuboid students can't cope with too much noise."

After Matron left, I noticed my qark, who was emitting a very high-pitched squeal as it yawned, at least an octave higher than the one I'd heard the previous evening. It looked very dishevelled and was licking its paws, rubbing its eyes, and from time to time rolling on its side and back.

"Good morning, Shin," I said, before pouring a bowl of popcorn.

As Shin snuffled at the food, I pulled on my Space Academy uniform. "I need to go and look for my dad," I said to Shin. "I know I'm not supposed to, but I have to find out what really happened to him. I have to know. I *have* to."

As I said these words, Shin's eyes began to turn red. Passion.

"Only problem," I continued, "I can't pilot a spacecraft because of my particular form of Rhuba. That means I'm going to have to find someone who will do it for me. And that means making friends, and I'm not good at that. In fact, I don't really like talking to people."

Shin looked at me inquisitively, then stood up, walked to the desk and curled up just beyond the chair, in the arch where my legs went. It seemed to know that I was about to leave and that its place was in my room, not in the canteen and the classrooms. Matron had told me last night, "You can't take a qark into a room full of people, like a classroom, or a lecture hall. They experience what we call empathic overload. There are so many emotions in the room that they become dazed and dizzy, and the colours in their eyes become fragmented, like a kaleidoscope."

"What happens to him while I'm at school?" I'd asked.

"Shin will stay in your room. Don't worry. Qarks are quite happy to take a break from absorbing other people's feelings. It's very tiring. They like the downtime and they don't mind being on their own."

"Me too," I said.

I said goodbye to Shin, feeling jealous of the creature being able to stay behind, and left my room, heading down a light grey walled corridor past square-shaped rooms until I found myself in an enormous oval chamber, with portraits of former Guardians on the walls. A huge chandelier hung from the high ceiling, with long sparkling limbs that drooped down from a glowing hood like the multicoloured tentacles found in the Ocean Nebula.

A crowd of students was lining up in front of an arched entrance to the dining hall. Even a quick look told me that there were many Rhuboid children. Some were stimming, rocking forwards and backwards to calm themselves, or flicking their fingers behind their backs. Others were in hoverchairs, unable to move their upper bodies or their limbs. A few had hands and fingers so twisted that even operating these vehicles was difficult.

My calculation was that about half the school was composed of students with unique needs. The other half was made up of people who were, at least on the surface of it, non-Rhuboid, although people argue whether this is even possible. My father used to say that there are far more people on the Rhuba spectrum than are formally diagnosed. "Most artists and scientists have a dash of Rhuba," he had said. So, who knows?

All I do know is that this school believed in integrating students with and without Rhuba. Gone were the days when schools had isolation cubicles for children with what used to be called "behavioural difficulties". These days, we referred to "differences" rather than "difficulties", and all schools practised integration not isolation. As if to underline the point, a banner hung above the entrance of the canteen. "Neurodiversity Rules!" it read.

As the queue moved on, I saw that breakfast was being served by the droids I'd met last night. Pancakes were on the menu and the droids were tossing each one in the air. I watched one girl, about twelve years old and on the low functioning end of the spectrum, suppress a giggle as her breakfast landed with a slapping sound on her plate. She nodded when the droid pointed to the honey option, and she muted another giggle when it drew what looked like a gun from a holster and fired the golden liquid onto her plate.

When it was my turn, I decided to try the Engorian syrup. The droid switched to its other holster and squirted a shot of the auburn coloured sauce onto my pancake. Some of it missed and hit me on the hand, which I raised and licked. Its sweetness shocked and then delighted me the instant it touched my tongue. I had never tasted anything like it before, not even when my mother made pancakes for me when I was little.

As I left the line, I started to walk towards the 24 long tables in the canteen, each one painted in a different pastel colour. I was about to sit at an empty space when an older girl approached and beckoned me to follow her. She had long auburn hair, pale skin and pronounced freckles. She was about the same height as me and walked without any difficulty. No sign of Rhuba. She seemed to have an air of confidence.

We arrived at a light, yellow table where she stopped. She pointed to her name label. It read, "Limeena Say."

I pointed to my lapel, showing my name, and she nodded. Then she gestured to me to sit and eat while she drew up a chair.

Limeena produced her communications pad and was about to show me something on its screen when there was uproar in the canteen. I turned to my right to see what was happening. It didn't take a genius to work it out. The chefbot from the kitchen had appeared and was standing in the serving area. It was still sporting a wig, lipstick and two droopy, plastic breasts. Most of the students couldn't contain themselves. The "no noise" rule went out of the window. Everyone was laughing, apart from a few children who were holding their hands over their ears.

The next second, Matron appeared. She stood on a raised platform at the end of the dining hall and thrust her hands on her hips. Shaking back a curl of brown hair, she stared into the crowd of students, looking this way and that, as if she knew already who was guilty.

"Who among you little darlinks is responsible for this?"

Silence.

"Own up!" Matron said.

More silence.

"Now!"

There was the shuffling of feet.

"If the culprit doesn't confess, the lot of you will spend an hour here after school, in detention."

Yet more silence.

"One last chance!"

A hand began to appear above a cluster of heads at a table to my left. The arm it belonged to was chubby, very chubby, and the torso the arm belonged to was… well… let's just say it looked like it had consumed all the pancakes in the entire canteen.

I focused for three seconds on the boy's head. Black hair. Large round face with flushed cheeks. Thick, puckering lips, pursing almost imperceptibly into a mischievous smile. Big black eyes, staring ahead, away from Matron, away from the chefbot.

I guessed he was about a year older than me.

"Sorry, Matron!" he said. His voice, which had half broken, was at least twice as loud and half as sincere as it should have been.

"Detention again for you, Loois."

There was muffled laughter at the mention of the boy's name. I was later to learn that no one called him Loois. He had two nicknames: The Impersonator and Thunder Butt, the second on account of winning "the loudest fart competition" every year since boarding at the Beacon. Most famously, he had stored a year's supply of gas from his farts in a homemade energy converter, and the rumour was he had powered a small rocket with it.

"That's the second time this week," Matron said, shaking her head.

Matron sighed, told all of us to finish our food, then walked out of the canteen through the serving area, commanding her mechanical lookalike to follow her. As soon as she had gone, Limeena pushed her pad in front of me, pointing to the screen. I turned the device so that I could read a short article, no longer than a page, entitled "Mentoring Protocols," with the Space Academy header above it.

"Every new student is given a mentor to help them adjust to the new challenges of life in our Space Academy. This mentor is an older student, usually in their final year, who takes on the role of guide and advisor, helping the new, younger student to integrate. In the case of Rhuboid students, this mentor acts as a translator, interpreting the physical signals from the younger pupils in their care.

We like to think of the Space Academy as a family, with mentors performing the role of older brothers and sisters.

If you are reading this, it is because your mentor has just introduced themselves to you.

We hope you will benefit from the caring oversight of your older brother or sister during your first year.

Be brave and be strong.

The Guardian."

I nodded to signal that I'd finished reading and Limeena took the pad back, allowing me to eat my succulent pancake. Then she passed the device back to me and pointed again to the screen. There was a picture of her in a pilot's uniform. Her bio was underneath.

"LIMEENA SAY:

"Limeena, 17, enrolled on the pilot training programme at the Academy when she was ten years old. By the time she was twelve, she had learned in a simulator how to fly. By fourteen, she had passed all her theory exams and by sixteen, she was the youngest person in the history of the Academy to graduate as a pilot. Limeena regularly flies in the co-pilot's seat and will be automatically authorised to fly solo on her eighteenth birthday."

I pushed the pad back to Limeena and mouthed one question. "When are you eighteen?"

"Two months," she whispered.

I was so excited, I almost smiled.

As it drew nearer, I could see that it was covered in spotted, oily skin, protected in places by armour plating where its bones had grown out of its skin to protect itself from predators.

6
Meeting the Fascinator

After I had consumed all my pancake and syrup, Limeena took my plate and tray, then led me to the exit. We passed through the arched doorway, then down a long corridor with windows that looked up and out onto the square buildings outside, now doused by the warm lights pouring down on us from invisible gantries. Vehicles of all shapes and sizes were hovering outside entrances, collecting people to take them to their workplaces throughout the Space Academy. Many were in clusters, like my father's bees, going about their business with a focus and a purpose that seemed robotic and mechanical, and in some cases, probably was.

After a long walk, we came out of the corridor into a wide and open hall. Students were standing still in front of the biggest door I'd ever seen. It was like something out of one of the stories Dad used to tell about the fantastic fortresses of faraway places, yet to be discovered, and beyond the reach of satellites and searcher drones. It was two doors, in fact, with top halves that curved towards each other.

"The Hall of Spores," Limeena whispered. "It's only just been built. Everyone loves it."

I nodded. Dad had told me about this place.

"We all spend thirty minutes here now before our classes," Limeena said. "The purity of the spores is a very welcome, timely antidote to the polluted atmosphere on our planet."

I nodded again.

Somehow, knowing that I was about to enter a space that had come from Dad's imagination, fashioned by his own hands, made it feel as if he was not so far away after all.

Two seconds later, the two doors began to open inwards towards the chamber beyond, which was larger than the dining hall, and bathed in a blue light that allowed enough visibility for us to navigate a path to the reclining chairs within what looked like pods.

When I lowered myself into my chair, the material beneath me felt as soft as my mother's blankets. A smell filled my nostrils, like the whiff of damp walls and stagnant pools inside a cave. Then a sound. Like the lapping of water and the breaking of small waves upon a shore. I observed small clouds beginning to form around us as I lay there, moving ever so slowly towards each one of us, enveloping us in their mist, until we were invisible from each other. It all reminded me of something.

When the moist particles touched the tip of my tongue, I knew what it was. I was back in the Space Ranger two nights ago, waiting for my father to return. The same taste had been on my tongue then too. The taste of the spores released by the Creepers beneath the rocks. Only this time, the taste was weaker than it had been that night. Yet it still worked its magic. My body felt invigorated, my perception enhanced, my energy increased, as if my entire being was being upgraded.

Looking up, I saw that the ceiling of the chamber was now sprinkled with a thousand stars, flickering against a black expanse. As I watched the twinkling dots of light, I lost myself somewhere in that space between sleeping and waking. The hinterland where I have my deepest perceptions of reality, my furthest reaches of creativity.

How long I inhabited this mindful space, I do not know. Time seemed to decelerate. Space seemed to expand.

The next thing I knew, Limeena was standing over me, watching my eyes spring open.

"Time to go," she said.

Most of the students had already left. Only those on hoverchairs and with support frames were still in the chamber. As I stood, my legs seemed stronger, my breathing calmer.

"We're heading to the Fascinator," Limeena said. "I won't explain. Just wait and see."

Seven minutes later, we entered an enormous greenhouse in the shape of a pyramid, filled with fronds and fruits, trees and plants, all photosynthesized by surrogate sunlight and small, intermittent gusts which shot out from shower heads in the metallic rafters.

"Through here," Limeena said, as she pushed aside some lowering branches and found a path in the undergrowth.

Ten seconds later, I saw it slouching in a dried-up puddle under a Dhoobi tree. It was a lethargic cumbersome creature, with upper arms that were far longer than its short legs. When it saw me, it began to move towards me. I say "move", but it dragged itself by its arms extremely slowly across the ground. It was the least mobile and agile of creatures.

As it drew nearer, I could see that it was covered in spotted, oily skin, protected in places by armour plating where its bones had grown out of its skin to protect itself from predators. These armour plates covered its head, collarbones, shoulders, backbone, elbows, hands and knees. The plates had skin as well, but it was more like leather than bone.

The armour on its face, around the eyes, ran down to the bottom of its chin. Its top teeth had grown out of its skin and were now protruding downwards, fully covering its mouth. I could see that it had to position itself underneath overhanging leaves and fruit to eat them, putting them in its mouth under the armour plating, using its strange hands.

I say "hands", in fact, the Fascinator had big hard knuckles and three fingers – a larger middle finger, resembling two small ones fused together – and two others either side. Its feet were the same shape, only there was a small thumb on the back of both heels.

As the Fascinator stopped a few paces away from me, it turned slightly, revealing a shell-like back. I could tell how important it was for the creature to have its back covered with the thickest and largest armour. Even watching it now, I could see how long it took to turn around, and how vulnerable its back would have been to an apex predator in the wild.

I had heard of these creatures. Everyone on Kel had. They came from the tropical forests of Rimda in the southern hemisphere of our planet and had been discovered by a scientist and explorer named Zagonda. She had found a dead specimen and dissected the bumps on its back, discovering that these wart-like lumps were in fact a very advanced and sensitive array of sensors. They had been named the Ampullae of Zagonda after her.

A short while later, Zagonda had rescued an infant Fascinator from certain death and brought it on board her ship to bring home. The story goes that she was dozing one day on the ship when the creature, who thought she was her mother, started to communicate with her through its ampullae. Somehow, she understood it all and then set about finding others who could interpret the creature's signals. These gifted people she called Receivers, of which she was the first and the most famous.

"Is this the one Zagonda brought back?" I asked.

"Yes," Limeena replied. "It's thought to be over 500 years old."

I gasped.

Zagonda's creature sat forwards, crouching on its short hindlegs, resting its rotund belly on the ground. For a while, it peered into me through the two black horizontal pupils in the centre of its eyes. Then the Receiver stepped forward from the trees.

I was surprised to see that the Receiver was a child, no more than eight years old, with a shaved head and bright blue eyes. She wore a long white robe and walked in bare feet. As the creature next to her began to communicate, the tiny lumps on its back began to throb with light and the Receiver's eyes went pale, as if a membrane had covered them.

"You are Khali," she said, her pale lips quivering as if she spoke. She looked as if she was in a trance.

I nodded, unsure whether to bow or not, ignorant of the etiquette for addressing a Fascinator.

The creature blinked twice and then stared at me, tapping the ground with the middle finger of one of its hands. As it continued to tap, I studied the dark marbling on its cream belly, and counted the different colours of the bumpy warts on its back – yellow, red, brown, black. They were now shining intermittently. Now that it was closer, I could smell the dirt that had attached itself to his entire body like space barnacles.

As I peered into the pitch-black lenses of its eyes, the creature's two nostrils opened wide and began to sniff me. After three sniffs, it shook its entire trunk, as if shocked by something.

"This one is wise beyond his years," the girl said, transmitting the creature's words. "He truly is his father's son."

"What do you see?" I asked.

The creature gulped down the last of the juices from a piece of fruit that had dropped on the ground.

The girl began to speak again. "I see a boy who is interested in many things but fascinated by only a few."

The creature paused.

"Such as?" I asked.

"Such as studying mathematical and geometrical patterns, particularly ones involving six-sided shapes, his beloved hexagons."

I gulped.

"Such as interpreting puzzles and enigmas, like the hieroglyphs on the stone tablet he received from his father. A puzzle that he will solve much sooner than he thinks."

I gulped even louder.

"Such as finding a light shining in a great cave."

I thought my epiglottis was going to leap out of my throat.

"He is treading in the footsteps of his father, fulfilling his father's dreams, and a destiny that is his very own."

The creature looked at me, its eyes staring and blinking, its ampullae shifting from one vivid colour to another.

Then the girl spoke. "We will design a path for him to follow so that he can pursue his fascinations."

Exhausted by its exertions, the creature fell into a deep sleep, snoring so loudly that the ground shook.

"Time to go," Limeena whispered.

I was about to turn and follow her, when something caught my eye. Un-derneath a Lobi tree, from deep within the shadowy recess beneath its overhanging branches and drooping leaves, something caught the light pouring in through the glass panels of the pyramid, from the sun blaz-ing above and beyond the great dome of the Academy.

Something gold.

It looked like a large medallion.

An engraved medallion.

"Wait!" I said to Limeena. "There's someone there."

Limeena pulled me by my sleeve. "Even more reason to go," she said, her face set like flint towards the exit.

On the way out, Limeena stopped at the desk in the air-conditioned atrium and picked up the instructions for my education in the form of a scroll. I untied the light blue ribbon and unfurled the parchment. It read, "Khali is to be put on an accelerated programme of science and engineering, under the tutelage of Professor Rondo Kinzi."

"Kinzi!" I said, my heart beating fast.

That was a name I knew well. Kinzi was a famous and eccentric genius. He had developed a new device for Rhuboid children, enabling them to become more spatially aware. He had used something he had discovered within the brain itself, a grid-based system in which a person establishes their position and navigates their way to a new location. He found that the brain uses *location cells* to establish position, and *navigation cells* to map a course. This grid looks like a hexagonal array. For navigating a large space, one hexagonal grid is added to another, and then to another, and so on, until a course has been set. Kinzi had argued in a now famous lecture that the brain maps other courses in the same way, such as the progression of abstract thoughts. Most impressive of all, Kinzi had created a software programme using this model and had given children with Rhuba a whole new awareness of space and movement.

"I can't believe it!" I cried.

"You're a very lucky boy," Limeena said. "Many people consider him to be the greatest living thinker. The very least you can say about him is that he has a brain the size of Kel."

"I know!"

"I suppose you want to know when you start his class."

I nodded.

"Tomorrow."

"Why not today?"

"The Professor is delivering an important address this afternoon about opening new portals to Xona. You can watch a playback of it in your room tonight, before you go to sleep."

"What do you mean 'new portals'?" I asked.

Limeena sighed. "It seems that one of the Ahketans has been pushing for a weapon to be developed that can blast new holes in Xona's upper atmosphere. The Ahketans have asked Professor Kinzi to draw up the design for such a weapon. He is not happy about that, not happy about it all."

I shuddered. If that happened, I knew what the consequences might be. Every mining vessel on Kel would head through the newly formed openings, down towards Xona, discovering the movements of the Creeper, exploiting the riches of the spores.

It would be an invasive and violent operation.

The violation of an entire planet.

Like the violation of Kel, at the beginning of our recorded history, the consequences of which everybody now experienced and suffered.

Dad had been right.

It was only a matter of time.

And time was running out.

Fast.

7
A Shadow Falls

For the rest of that morning, Limeena showed me around the classrooms, lecture theatres and laboratories of the Space Academy, then, in the afternoon, accompanied me to a series of tests designed to find how smart I was in various subjects and activities. These lasted until the evening meal in the canteen, where I was grateful for the silence.

When I returned to my room with Limeena, Shin was sitting upright, its back legs protruding from the side of my bed, front legs tucked into its furry chest, belly drooping downwards towards its knees. When it saw me, it fell forward from the bed onto the floor and rolled onto its back, emitting yelps of pleasure. Then it stared at me, its eyes turning grey.

"It thinks you're strong," Limeena said, looking at the colour chart on the wall above my bed.

In truth, I felt weak. More than that, I felt sad. Looking at the sparsely furnished room and the bare white walls, I longed for my old bedroom, my bedclothes, my toys, my belongings. I yearned for my mother's love and ached for my father's voice. For the first time in my life, I was homesick for my father and my home, and Shin's grey eyes had discerned it because with one swift movement, it – no, *he* – was at my side, nestling into my lap, making the cutest sounds I had ever heard, turning my sadness into smiles.

As Limeena made to leave, she caught sight of the stone tablet. "Is that what the Fascinator mentioned?"

"No more questions!" I cried, holding my head in my hands.

"That's okay," Limeena said. "You can show me tomorrow. Sleep well. And don't forget Professor Kinzi's lecture."

I undressed, hung up my uniform, washed my face and brushed my teeth. I then put on my pyjamas, took my new school pad and climbed into bed. As Shin nestled under my arm, I switched on the device and found the news item. A young woman in a sleek, silver dress was reporting from outside the Parliament building in the heart of Kailorian, our capital city.

"Professor Rondo Kinzi has today indicated that there isn't much time left before the opening to Xona's upper atmosphere seals itself shut forever," the silvery woman said. The piece then cut to the address. Kinzi, a lean man in his seventh decade and with the same coloured skin as my father, was standing at a glass lectern with the Space Academy logo emblazoned on it. He had grey spikes of hair that looked like the icy stalagmites I had once seen in a picture of the caves of Goram. Although his hair was mad, his words were far from insane. They were measured, reasoned and calm.

"The only opening to the world of Xona is closing," he said, squinting at the audience through tiny, gold-rimmed spectacles. "There are spores that rise from the planet's surface that we think are responsible for this. We have, in the last few days, discovered that these have the power to rejuvenate material. It seems the spores may now be healing the fracture caused by one of Xona's volcanoes. The closure of this doorway will be permanent."

The news cut back to the reporter.

"You could hear gasps right across the theatre when the Professor made these remarks," she said, a grave look on her face. "But after the gasps had died down, Professor Kinzi turned to a possible solution."

Cut back to the Professor's face.

"I have been asked to conduct tests on the force that caused the hole in the first place. I have measured the strength, direction and composition of the lava blast and, as requested by the Ahketans, have adapted our most advanced weapons so they can create a series of new holes. Once these openings are formed, it will be possible to establish mining facilities at the circumference of each hole, enabling us to continue importing the life-enhancing power of Xona's spores, should we choose to do that."

With that, the theatre experienced its own eruption as the audience stood. When the clapping had died down, the Professor concluded, "There are great and desperate needs on our planet, such as the need for new medical cures and new industrial technologies, to name but two. Too many of our people are still dying of incurable diseases and too much of our planet is dying too. In fighting these things, the spores of Xona provide us with a chance to pioneer new opportunities for sustainable and enriched life."

The Professor then withdrew his spectacles and placed them on the lectern. He leaned forward, looking into the camera with his piercing black eyes, his forehead furrowed. "But there will be an enormous cost to this," he said. "To save our own planet, we will need to plunder Xona's natural resources. I, for one, have moral questions about such an act."

Murmurs in the audience.

"We will be demanding the greatest of sacrifices from Xona," he said.

More murmurs.

"In former times, we referred to Xona as the Great Sister. Well, this will be like a sister giving up her life for her twin. Except with this difference..." He paused, waiting for complete silence. "The sister who lays down her life will not have chosen to do so. The other will have made this decision for her. And that, in any book, is questionable."

No one moved.

"This is a choice, ladies and gentlemen," he concluded. "We can blast holes in the upper atmosphere of our sister planet, robbing Xona of her life-giving energy. Or, we can seek another way."

There was a smattering of applause as the Professor withdrew from the stage, his shoulders hunched, his eyes sad.

As the news cut back to the reporter, I lay in bed thinking of the planet's fruitful trees and flowers wilting and fading in the unfiltered rays of the sun as they poured through the newly formed blast holes.

I switched off the report and commanded the light in my room to dim. I needed to hear my father's voice now, to know his heart, to lean upon his wisdom once again. I turned to the drawer beside my bed and took the white-framed pad I had brought home with me from the Doxana, the one on which my father's last transmission was recorded.

I heard him once again mentioning the cave and the tunnel, the lake and the light.

Then the coordinates.

Clear as the speech from the Parliament Building.

12

17

1

9

13

21

11
10
7
22
3
5
14
18
2
4
20
6
8
15
16
19
23
I listened to him repeating these numbers.
12
17
1
9
13
21
11
10
7
22
3
5
14

18

2

4

20

6

8

15

16

19

23!

When he reached the end the second time, I noticed something that I hadn't detected at the time of the original transmission.

He emphasised the final number.

Almost shouted it out.

Why did my father do that?

Then it hit me. The number of shapes on the stone puzzle he had given me for my birthday present… There were 23 of them.

I couldn't scramble out of bed fast enough. Kneeling in front of the stone, I ran my hand over the Lagentum plate, and the 23 shapes moved in response. I returned the shapes to their original order and then set to work. I began by attributing numbers to each of the shapes, in their chronological order, 1 to 23. Then I moved the first number Dad had mentioned, the number 12, into the space occupied by the shape with no 1 in my head. Then I put 17 into the second shape. 1 into the third shape, and so on, and so on, until, with a trepidation more intense than I had ever known, I moved the twenty third shape into its only remaining space.

As soon as I did, the lines separating the different shapes began to illuminate, as if filled with tiny streams of lava. Then the symbols began to illuminate too, changing this way and that, as in some intoxicating dance, until they morphed into letters which in turn formed a message, the message I had longed to hear from my father. As I read, my breathing became faster.

When the warbirds rise
And the towers fall,
You must break this stone
To save us all.

I scratched my head. What in Xona's name did that mean? It seemed that solving the puzzle had only served to create a new one. As I tried to work it all out, Shin became restless and the golden bangle around my wrist began to grow warm. As I tried to loosen the timepiece, I became aware of a tall, dark shadow standing outside the door. I could sense the shape of it, and feel its power, even without seeing it.

It seemed to be covered in what looked like black feathers.

And its head was enlarged, in the shape of a great bird.

It was terrifying.

Suffocating.

Growing larger.

Filling the corridor outside.

Seeping like black liquid underneath my door.

I turned back in desperation to my father's stone. The Time Keeper around my wrist seemed to be growing warmer and warmer, as if it was about to burn my skin. It was hot now. Beginning to hurt me.

I wrestled the strap from my wrist and hurled it to the floor, shouting "Leave me alone!" My voice seemed louder, deeper, stronger than I had ever known. Like a man's voice. A man with authority.

Suddenly, the shadow outside seemed to stop growing, as if it had stalled before reaching the summit of its strength. Little by little, it shrank and diminished, until it was reduced to the size of a mere man.

It waited outside my door.

Then it sloped away.

Until it disappeared altogether.

As the low-level lighting filled my room again, I reached out to the stone tablet and cried, "Dad!" There were tears filling my eyes and pouring down my cheeks. I could still see his message. And a part of it which I had not had time to read. Old, familiar words.

Me to you.

You to me.

Forever.

I sat for a long time, cross-legged in front of the stone, with Shin purring in my lap, until the tiredness overwhelmed me. I drew my hand over the Lagentum plate and restored the shapes and the hieroglyphs to their original, incoherent order. I climbed into bed and returned the white-framed pad to my drawer, but not before erasing the transmissions from my father. I had committed everything he said to memory anyway, including the 23 numbers, and I couldn't risk anyone else finding the device and hearing what I had heard. It was our secret.

As I lay there, with Shin under my arm, I realised that the numbers my father had shared were not the coordinates for finding the light in the cave on Xona. He knew that the light would draw me back one day anyway, and that I didn't need help finding the location. No, he had clearly dreamed of something to do with my future, Kel's future, something to do with the breaking out of war and the breaking of the stone.

More than that, I could not tell.

I felt so proud at finding the solution to the puzzle, but then my thoughts returned to the shadow outside my room.

Who was it?

What did it want?

And why did the Time Keeper, still lying on the floor, grow so hot around my wrist? Was it really a watch or a clock? Was it just a device for recording time and forming a story? Or was it some sort of motion detector that reacted to the approach of a sinister and dangerous presence?

I would have gone on asking such questions, and no doubt increasing my anxiety, except that Matron walked past and knocked on my door, scolding me for still being up.

"Lights out, darlink," she called.

Sleep proved hard to find that night. All I could think of was the shadow that had appeared at my door and the words that had appeared on my father's stone tablet.

What were these warbirds and who was flying them?

What towers was Dad referring to?

And why would I need to break the stone to save the world?

8
The Class of 24

Early next morning, the questions were still bombarding my mind. Even with the heightened perception and intelligence gained from my close contact with Arokah, I was still finding it difficult to know what was really going on and who I could trust.

Just after Matron's morning call, Limeena came to escort me to breakfast and lessons. As she walked into my room, Shin's eyes lit up with a deep purple colour. I glanced at the chart. Negative purple means arrogant, cocky, proud. I knew she wasn't any of those things. Positive purple means royal, noble, confident. That was more like it. Limeena had an air about her, like one who was not easily flustered, one who managed her moods well, one who kept her head when others, like mine, were spinning.

"I'm happy you're here, Limeena," I said.

She smiled, bent down towards Shin, and stroked the creature, who I could see had decided to become male, rubbing his chin against the soft white skin of her hand, purring and flirting without shame.

"I love your qark," she said.

"I think he loves you," I said.

As Shin's eyes turned yellow, I turned back towards the colour chart. Negative yellow, unstable. That wasn't right. Limeena was the most stable person I'd met so far. Even her gait when she stood, and her posture when she sat, looked like the Rock of Dalarion. It had to be positive yellow. *Happy.* That's more like it. Limeena, I could already tell, was not one for showing her emotions, but there was a trace of a smile on her face.

Just then, Limeena looked at the stone tablet, standing by the wall. She glanced at the strange shapes and symbols, which had been reset to their original, mysterious configuration the night before.

"Can you tell me what this is?" she asked.

I thought for ten seconds. Could I share my secret with her? I looked into Shin's eyes. They were still shimmering with a yellow colour. No hint of concealment, betrayal, deception or darkness. In fact, I almost felt as if Shin had transferred his loyalties to her, a feeling that was met by a glance from Shin, whose eyes had turned green. I didn't have to consult the wall chart to know what that meant.

Jealousy!

"It's the gift my father gave me."

"May I look at it?"

I nodded, and she knelt in front of the stone. When she touched the Lagentum plate, two things happened, neither of which I had been expecting. The first was that she twitched, as if someone had tickled the tiny hairs on the nape of her neck. The second was that the shapes on the plate moved in response to her hand.

"That's odd," I said. "I thought I was the only one who was able to move the pieces like that."

Limeena said nothing. She kept moving both her hands, like the conductor of the Academy's orchestra, as if every movement was producing new resonances, new melodies.

"What happened when you touched it?" I asked.

"It was like I had been connected to an energy source," she answered. "I felt a surge of strength. It went right through my hand, into my shoulder, and then travelled from my head to my toes. I feel as if I could run and never stop. I've never experienced anything like it."

I nodded as Limeena continued to reposition the pieces, trying to discover the patterns in the puzzle. "It's a great present," she said. "It would take me many moons to even begin to solve it. I presume the shapes with the symbols on them are meant to fit the pattern? Have you worked it out yet?"

I paused, looking at Shin who was staring at Limeena's long, ginger hair. "Can you keep a secret?" I asked.

She looked away from the stone and sat facing me, her face calm, but her eyes sad. "I had to keep many secrets when I was a child," she said.

"What kind of secrets?"

Limeena was struggling with her words."My father ... he wasn't nice to me ... he hit me ... a lot ... until he was discovered. But even then ... I never betrayed him. He betrayed himself. When Mum found out ... she left him, he was put in prison, and I was sent here, when I was eight years old."

"Is your mother still alive?"

Limeena shook her head.

"Have you seen your father since he's been in prison?"

Limeena shook her head again. She looked down at the floor, as if reliving some terrible trauma, before taking control again, looking at me. "I'm not ready for that. I would need to forgive him first, and that's much easier said than done."

She sighed and bowed.

Then I sat in silence, looking at Shin, whose eyes were a sullen grey, and whose nose was now nudging Limeena's leg.

Then Limeena looked up at me. "I have one other secret," she said. "One no one else knows."

She lifted her pale hands to her head and thrust her freckled fingers into her auburn hair. The next second, her hair was off her head, revealing a bald, pale scalp, dappled by faint, grey blotches.

"I have Grooda's Syndrome," she said. "Had it since I was your age. One day, my hair just started to fall out in clumps. Not everywhere. Just in the places where the lighter patches are."

"I'm sorry."

"Don't be. Of course, it was embarrassing at first. I used to have lovely auburn hair, and when it started falling out, well, that was upsetting. But after a while, I started wearing this Bandorian hairpiece. It gave me a new confidence. Now I'm just happy with who I am."

Limeena picked up the matt of auburn hair on her lap and placed it back on her head. "I just wanted to share my secrets with you, so you know that you can trust me. I'm on your side, Khali. Always. And you're not alone. I'm your mentor. In time, I hope I'll be your friend."

Limeena turned back to the stone, then looked at me. "If you don't want to share your secret with me, let's leave it."

That was when I knew I could trust her.

I began telling her what my father and I had done, how Dad had followed the light, gone missing in the cave, how I had returned home, then been told by two officers that I was coming to the Beacon and last of all, how I had discovered the message in the puzzle last night.

I recited the strange verse from the tablet.

"My father was beginning to have strange dreams about the future," I said. "But I don't know that even he understood what it meant."

Then I told Limeena about the golden Time Keeper that had burned my wrist, and the shadow at my door last night, trying to enter my room, trying to access the stone, or so I thought.

"Others are clearly interested in this," she said. "Its power is immense. I can feel it, this close to it. It sounds from your father's words on the stone as if he thinks – sorry, he thought – that there will be a war in the future. And that the stone will somehow be important."

I nodded.

"Do you have any idea why?"

"I really don't know. The only clue is a dream I've been having about my father. I keep seeing him deep within the cave on Xona, pointing to the light pouring from deep within the cave, then pointing to the stone he gave me, as if there's some connection between the two that I've not yet seen. It's one of the reasons I want to go back there, not just to find out what happened to Dad, but to take his tablet with me, and see what happens when I bring it into closer contact with the light."

"Flying back to Xona isn't going to be easy," Limeena said. "In fact, it couldn't really be more difficult."

"Maybe you could help me," I said.

She laughed.

"You're going to be graduating soon," I continued. "And everyone says you're the best young pilot in the fleet."

"I'd like to help you," she said as she stood. "But I would need time to think about that. I could lose everything. My license. My career. My freedom. Even my life. It's not a decision I could take lightly."

"But Limeena," I said. "you know there's no way I can fly. How else can I get there?"

Everyone on our planet, including Limeena, knew that children and young people with a certain kind of Rhuba weren't allowed to pilot space vehicles. There was no unkindness behind this ruling. It was because people with my form of Rhuba can freeze in traumatic situations. Pilots need to be cool in a crisis. Cool is one thing. Frozen is quite another.

"It's complicated," she replied.

"Please, Limeena!"

"I won't promise anything," she said. "I won't rule it out either. I just need some time."

"That's what we don't have," I said, picking up the Time Keeper from my bedside table and flinching. Anxious that it would burn me again, I thrust it in the pocket of my Space Academy jacket as Limeena stood.

"Breakfast," she said, patting Shin on his nose.

After eating my syrupy waffles, I walked with Limeena from the canteen out into the oval chamber beyond. As we stood there for a few minutes, I saw Demorah across the crowded room, standing on her own, looking at some faces on a video monitor on the wall.

"I met her," I said, pointing to Demorah.

"She's a pilot too," Limeena said.

"I know. She flew me here. She hardly said a word."

"She's become very quiet lately," Limeena said.

"Is there something wrong with her?" I asked.

"Look, Khali. Every pupil at the Beacon shares one thing in common. We are all orphans. Either our mums and dads are dead, or they're in prison, or they're just somewhere else. And the thing about us orphans is this, we all react to our loss differently. Some of us hunger for friendship, desperate for a love that we have lost. Others of us avoid friendship, terrified that we will lose someone all over again."

Limeena pointed to her long, flowing head of hair and smiled at me. "We are all covering things up," she said. "But the key thing is to share your secrets with someone you trust, because when you find someone to share your heart with, then you're no longer alone."

"Can I trust her?" I asked.

"Why do you ask that?"

"Because if you won't be my pilot, maybe she will."

Just then, Demorah saw me across the hall. She half waved, then turned around and hurried out of one of the doors, mingling with a group of cadets until she disappeared from our view.

We followed in the wake of the departing students, exiting the Beacon and heading out into the sun-soaked campus. As we walked down a long, gravelled path, I took out my Time Keeper.

"Are you frightened of wearing that?" Limeena asked.

"It hurt me last night."

"Why do you think that was?"

"I don't know. Maybe it's connected to the shadow. Maybe it's a device for inflicting pain when people don't do what the shadow wants."

Limeena didn't respond straightaway. She seemed to be thinking. Then she said, "It's not the only possibility."

"What do you mean?"

"Maybe it contains some kind of warning system, alerting you when the shadow is near."

"I had thought that too," I said. "But it still hurt me."

"Well, there may be an explanation for that too," Limeena said.

We hurried on, passing a science block on our left and an engineering facility on our right, both designed in the standard rectilinear shapes that I had seen everywhere – massive white blocks with straight lines and right angles. The only relief to this monotonous design were the two lines of bright green Bornai trees each side of us, and the crystal-clear pond at the end of the avenue, home to three ornamental Messimi fish.

The Academy Headquarters appeared as we cleared the trees. It rose high and proud above us – a tower-shaped building on a great stone base, with enormous, square windows in steel frames.

We climbed the forty-five marble steps that led up to the six sets of revolving doors at the foot of the tower – three on the left for entering, three on the right for leaving.

Once inside the atrium, my eyes were drawn to a stone sculpture standing in the middle of the limestone floor. It featured a twenty-foot high Messimi fish with water pouring from its thick-lipped mouth into a circular pool beneath. The surface of the water was shimmering under the lights, and some of the students were standing around it, staring into the trembling liquid. It glowed with the same soothing serenity that had washed over me earlier that morning in the Hall of Spores. Several of the students were rocking from side to side in a gentle motion as they stood beside the pool. One was spinning slowly, her arms stretched out like a bird's.

"This way," Limeena said.

I followed her into a glass lift which rose through another sculpture, this time a waterfall, into the heights of the fifty-storey building. Through the gaps in the streams of water I could see beyond the Academy to the mighty dome that protected the entire landscape. The sound of the falling water, clearly audible above the silent motor of the lift, made me so relaxed that I thought I was going to fall asleep. The only thing that roused me was Limeena's voice. She was the only other person besides me in the lift.

"Seeing as you shared your secret with me, and I with you," she said softly. "You can call me Meena. That's what my friends call me, and I'd like you to become my friend."

"Okay, Meena," I said.

The lift came to a halt at the fiftieth floor and we walked out onto a long corridor, with windows looking out onto the avenue of trees on one side, and onto classrooms and lecture halls on the other.

We stopped at a door with the number 24 on it, and Professor Rondo Kinzi's name underneath. I had noticed all the other numbers in the sequence of rooms were in order: 1, 2, 3, 4, 5, 6, and so on. Except that we had jumped from 7 to 24, before returning to 8. I pointed this out to Meena.

"I'm in the Professor's class as well," Meena said before she opened the door. "I'm pupil number 23. With you, there are now 24 of us. That brings us up to full strength."

Just before we walked in, she added, "We are the Class of 24."

9
My Father's Bees

As soon as Meena and I walked into the classroom, 22 students glanced round at us, then swivelled back so that they were facing Professor Kinzi, who had just entered through a side door. Everyone stood. When he sat, everyone sat. Except Meena and me.

"Ah," the Professor said, his chiselled face breaking into a smile. "I see we are now up to 24. Please take your seat."

He pointed towards an empty white chair at the back, standing vacant in front of a desk with silver-coloured, metal legs. It was situated next to the side wall of the classroom, underneath a window. There was a remote device with coloured buttons attached to the table by a black, spiral wire. A screen stood upright at the front of the desk, already activated.

Meena sat down at the front.

As I approached my seat at the back, I passed a large boy with thick black hair and freckles. I hadn't recognised him. Facial recognition had always been a bit of a problem for me.

He leaned over towards me and placed what looked like a small mask over his mouth. It was made of copper-looking metal and had tiny buttons and multi-coloured lights on it. After pressing one of the buttons, the boy spoke through the mask. "Welcome to the Class of 24, young man." The lights flashed as he spoke, as if in tune with his voice.

I jolted. The boy sounded exactly like the Professor.

"It's my invention," the boy said. "I can impersonate anyone with this thing. Clever, huh?"

As he spoke with his own voice again, I recalled the previous morning. The mischievous boy in the canteen. Matron's anger at him. The laughter of almost all the students. Suddenly, I understood why Thunder Butt was also called The Impersonator.

"Silence now," Kinzi said.

The Professor stood and faced an ageing blackboard whose wooden borders were pitted and rough. As the sun poured through the windows, one of its rays cast a white patch on the dark surface. As the Professor noticed the splash of light blemishing his board, he picked up an eraser about the size of his hand. It was wooden on one side and had a felt-like material on the other. He reached up to the top left corner and started rubbing the patch furiously. There was a murmur of laughter around the class.

I, meanwhile, marvelled at the pointlessness of the action.

How could someone so smart be so stupid?

Then I remembered something my father had said.

"Most of the people who teach at the Academy are absent-minded professors who probably have a hint of Rhuba, undiagnosed of course. One day you'll see. They can be very strange. But they are brilliant, just like you, my little professor."

As I was remembering this, the sun disappeared behind some clouds and the white patch disappeared with it. Seeing that his board was unblemished, the Professor picked up a white pen and began to write.

"KHALI BABACO."

My name.

"We have a celebrity in our midst," the Professor said in a sombre tone. "The son of the late, great Babaco."

Everyone had heard of my father. Everyone was familiar with his achievements. The Professor had called him the finest scientist of our generation. I had heard this mentioned in the news, after my father was announced as missing, presumed dead.

"Khali, let me introduce you to your peers. This is the Class of 24. You have joined a very select group. Almost half of the class members are Rhuboid, like you. The others are non-Rhuboid, like Limeena, whom you already know. You are among the top 24 students not just in the Beacon, but in the entire Academy. Congratulations."

Everyone in the class stood, smiled, removed their Space Academy caps and then clapped in perfect unison, starting slowly, then accelerating until the clap was as fast as the sound of an unmuted waterfall. Even Thunder Butt was smiling, although I was nervous of another blast from his bottom, which was far too close to my face for my liking.

"Now, then, Khali," the Professor said, when everyone had sat down. "It's your turn to stand."

I rose from my desk. I felt vulnerable, as if everyone was looking at me. Except that they weren't. The Professor had them all look straight ahead, at the blackboard, which had turned into a glass screen.

"Take out your school pad, please."

I withdrew the device from my utility belt.

"I assume it has all your work stored on it?"

"Yes, Professor."

"Well then, please share with the class something you've been working on in your own time, something that you've figured out for yourself, something that … fascinates you."

Silence fell.

I thought about what the Fascinator had said, then pressed the touch-sensitive screen on my device, typing my password with my thumbs, then locating a file with the index finger of my right hand. I pushed the Network Connect icon, and the screen at the front of the class lit up, revealing a hive of bees, all busy in and around their honeycomb.

"These are my father's bees," I said. Then, self-editing my words, I added, "*were* my father's bees."

As I looked at the screen, I remembered that there had been 153 bees in my father's hive. Each bee was the size of my little finger and had six shiny black eyes, three on each side of its face. Each one also had red, yellow and black markings on their backs. Three wings trembled each side of its spiracle-shaped abdomen, making six in all – two forewings, two mid wings, two hind wings. Dad always used to say that angels had six wings, so he called them his "Little Angels".

"Six legs, six wings, six eyes," I said, almost as if the class wasn't there. "The Endorian honeybee likes the number six."

The camera focused on the honeycomb.

"The bees shape their hive with the help of their telekinetic tongues," I said, "and these appear to work in unison, creating the same patterns, the same shapes, the same fundamental design."

Images of the pattern, close-up, appeared on the screen. Golden shapes, radiating, glowing, shimmering.

I continued, "Perhaps you can see the number six again, in the densely packed array of six-sided shapes, hexagonal shapes, made of beeswax. The tongues of all these extraordinary creatures seem to function in response to a kind of hive mind, creating a world that is remarkable for its economy and efficiency."

The picture on the screen now changed, from the honeycomb to falling snow on the Mountains of Drebar. There was a murmur from my classmates, and even Professor Kinzi seemed to break into a smile.

"Beautiful," he said.

More murmurs.

"Have you ever wondered how snow can become so compacted?" I asked. "Look at each snowflake. How unique. Different configurations, yes, but the same shape connects them all. The hexagon. Every snowflake is like a six-sided star. Even if each star has its own distinctive properties, its form has the structure of a hexagon. Ever asked yourself why? And how? Why is it that tiny drops of water, when they fall and freeze in mid-air, assume these patterns, based on hexagons?"

Professor Kinzi's smile widened.

"I'll tell you. It's because snowflakes on our planet are made up of molecules of water, and these molecules possess the structural elements necessary to create hexagonal patterns."

From there, I went on to describe the bubble rafts that form on the surface of the Sea of Dreams, covered by a soapy foam. I revealed how the bubbles are packed tightly together, each one morphing into a hexagonal shape, making the entire raft a hexagonal array.

Then I returned to the Mountains of Drebar, and to a dense cluster of tall, thin rocks well-known on our planet, again hexagonal in construction. I reminded my new classmates how molten lava contracts when it cools, creating a crack formation, which in turn makes a remarkable network of columns packed together in a hexagonal arrangement.

Before I finished, I showed images of our own skin tissue and DNA.

"We are carbon creatures," I said. "From our heads to our toes, there is carbon everywhere. And if you were to focus carefully, you'd see within this carbonite material many series of hexagonal chains, packed together with perfect efficiency, throughout our entire bodies."

I could see that my classmates were impressed.

"Much of this is a mystery," I said. "But what we do know is that this pattern forms because hexagonal shapes offer the most efficient packing system within our universe. When honeycombs and snowflakes, rock formations and bubbles, pack themselves together in these six-sided forms, there is no wasted space at all."

The Professor raised a hand, signalling to the class that he was not ready for them to applaud just yet.

"And what benefit might this provide to our planet?" he asked.

"Well, I've been thinking," I replied. "We all know that much of our planet is uninhabitable, and that those areas where we do build and live are limited in space."

There were nods in the room.

"Maybe we should look at developing nature's architecture. Maybe, if we want to use all the space with maximum efficiency and minimum waste, we should learn from my father's bees."

I paused before concluding.

"It seems to me that our world is trying to tell us something. Everywhere you look, if you have eyes to see, there is a pattern, hidden in plain sight, with the key to a new way of building, which is really an old way of building – a way as old as the rocks and the sea. I believe our universe is sending us a signal through its natural formations, a way to maximise what space we have, and to make our environment more pleasing to the eye."

The Professor was the first to applaud. Then everyone joined in. Meena was clapping the loudest at the front.

When the hubbub had died down, the Professor frowned. "There is something else you've discovered, isn't there?"

Suddenly, I felt anxious. Had the Professor somehow learned about the secret off-world mission undertaken by my father and me? Had he come to hear about the cave and the light? I had to share something, just enough to satisfy the Professor's curiosity.

"Yes," I said.

"And?"

"I have discovered an algorithm that no one has seen before. It's made up of hexagons. I'm not ready to talk about it yet, but it's a geometric structure that's foundational to our planet, one that will require a deeper maths than any of us have been used to if we're to understand it."

The Professor looked curious, and then content. "And that's all you're prepared to share for now?"

I nodded.

"And this is your fascination?"

"One of them."

"Well, we all look forward to hearing more about it, Khali." Then, addressing the students, he added, "Now, you can clap."

For the rest of the lessons that day, the Professor summarised the lecture he had given at the Parliament building, about mining the spores from Xona. He asked our opinions about the dangers posed by this operation, especially the ecological consequences. He shared that the seven Ahketans were divided about what to do, whether to blast holes in the upper crust of Xona's atmosphere or to find alternative ways of remedying the problems on our own world. He asked us what we would do.

For my part, I knew that perforating the upper crust of Xona's atmosphere would be risky. Sunlight would pour through this new, unprotected layer, signalling potential danger to the ecosystems on the planet, maybe even destroying its lush vegetation. Mining the spores might be destructive too, draining the energy from the planet, bringing an end to life on Xona while enriching, at least for a time, life on Kel.

Yet, I also knew that the one opening into Xona's world was closing, and that if other gateways weren't established, I might never find a way to return to the planet.

I was relieved when the Professor turned to Meena, and I was impressed by her answer.

"We must try to find a solution that is the best of both worlds and the best for both worlds," she said.

Everyone clapped. Well, almost everyone. Someone was not engaged with the discussion at all. As soon as I saw the grey hair, I guessed who it was. Demorah. So, she too was a member of the Class of 24. But she seemed distracted. Lonely, even in a crowd of people. And then I remembered what Meena had said in the oval chamber, loneliness is not having someone to share your heart with, and I thought to myself, "One day, Demorah, you will share your heart with me."

Before the lesson ended, Thunder Butt decided to perform a last prank. We could all see that the afternoon sun had come out, although none of its rays were passing through the window onto the blackboard. One, however, was shining directly at Thunder Butt, who was shielding his eyes as the Professor drew on the board, which was now black again.

Thunder Butt withdrew a small mirror from his desk and redirected the sun's ray towards the board, creating the same kind of white patch that he knew enfuriated the Professor. The old teacher, seeing the stain, leaned down and picked up the eraser. He started to wipe the patch as vigorously as his old arms were able, tutting and muttering as he did. Thunder Butt then started to move the mirror, causing the white patch to move from one side of the board to the other. As everyone in the classroom watched the Professor, I could hear a giggle or two, then a laugh, then more laughter, until almost everyone in the class was laughing so hard, they had tears in their eyes.

As the laughter grew, the Professor turned around and cast his eyes around the room. Thunder Butt was a little too slow hiding the glass. "Loois!" the Professor roared. "Detention!"

"But Professor, I already have a detention today, for Matron."

"You will do mine first."

The Professor put down the eraser. "The Class of 24 is now dismissed!" he shouted.

10
I Need to be Alone

To say that I was exhausted at the end of my first day of lessons would not be an exaggeration. My head was beginning to ache and my eyes were sore as the students left the room one by one, saying goodbye to the Professor, who was standing at the door at the back.

I pushed past Thunder Butt's back, flinching as I went, waiting for a guff that never came. Instead, I heard him whisper, "Sorry about impersonating the Professor, Khali. I can't help myself." I did not reply but made my way towards the Professor. I was the last person to exit.

As I passed him, the Professor tapped me on the shoulder. I turned but looked away from his face. I wished I had Shin with me. I sensed a sadness in his voice. "I'm very sorry about your father," he said. "You are very like him, both in physical appearance, and in intellect."

"Thank you," I said.

"Maybe," he continued, "some afternoon after school, we could have some hot chocolate and jam-filled truffins, and I can tell you what I knew of him and his work."

"I would like that," I said.

"Tomorrow? I'll tell the Guardian that you're excused your evening meal. Bring Limeena, if it would help you."

"Okay," I said, leaving the room.

"What did he say?" Meena asked as I entered the corridor. She had been waiting for me. All my other classmates had run off to the lifts, eager to get outside and relax while there was still some light.

"Please, Meena," I said, my head in my hands. "I have a headache. No more questions for now."

Meena said nothing. Just nodded.

"I'm going to have some time to myself. I just can't cope with any more noise, any more words."

Meena nodded again.

I left her outside the classroom and made my way down to the atrium and out through the doors. I walked all the way down the avenue of trees, avoiding the other students, and did my fast walk all the way back to my room.

Shin could sense my mood. Instead of living up to its name by rubbing its dishevelled flanks against my calves, Shin pulled away, waiting to see where I would go. There were very few options in my room. The only place I could retreat was my built-in wardrobe. This appealed to me because it was an enclosed space, with the walls within touching distance of my body. And the clothes that hung from the railing above draped over my shoulders and arms, creating the sensation of being enfolded and protected.

I opened it, sat beneath the garments, watched Shin, then closed the door again. There I sat, my face resting on my knees, slowing my breathing – inhaling for six seconds, exhaling for six seconds, doing so three times, while with the index finger of my right hand I pressed down on the palm of my left, drawing a six sided shape, three times once again.

I repeated my calming strategy.

Then I did it again.

Just as I was beginning to relax, I heard the door to my room hiss. I peered through the lattice door, while the arms of my father's ceremonial uniform were draped around my shoulders.

Someone was in my room. I could see Shin sitting on my bed looking at him or her. Its eyes were trained on the shifting shape, but I couldn't see what colour they were.

For several seconds, I thought maybe it was Matron, come to change my bed, or leave some clean laundry.

Then I saw it.

The glint of light on a gold medallion. That same refraction, same pendant, that I had seen in the Fascinator's Greenhouse. It was the Guardian, and he was rifling through the drawer beside my bed.

He found the white-framed pad from the Doxana and pressed the switch. There was a crackling noise. The recording of my father's transmissions had been erased. I breathed a sigh of relief.

Then he picked up my father's silver pad. He tried guessing the password. He did this several times, then gave up. I sighed again, but too soon. He withdrew a small stick from his studded belt and inserted it in one of the ports on the side. The screen illuminated again and this time the Guardian, who had bypassed my father's security protocols, was in and the crystal shapes hovering over his shoulders and forehead started to shimmer.

I could see him clearly now through the gaps in the lattice. His face was fixed and greedy like a bounty hunter, his hands moving over the screen with speed, his fingers pressing on icons and files, one after another, tapping away faster than I could ever imagine doing.

He cursed several times, which told me that he'd been frustrated in his search. Maybe he had tried to open the file I had accessed just last night, only to find it erased. Or perhaps he'd found what he was looking for, but it was encrypted by my cautious father, delaying his prying eyes from seeing some text. Or maybe the long, straggly black hair covering his ears prevented him from listening to audio files altogether.

But then a smile broke out on his stubble covered face, revealing several gold lines filling the cracks in the top and bottom rows of his teeth at the front of his mouth.

He pressed down on the screen and I heard my father's voice.

"Journal date, 24th day, Lunar Month 3, Year 2457."

That was just three days ago, the day before he disappeared.

The Guardian sat deeper onto my bed, his back leaning against the wall, my father's silver pad cradled in his lap. Shin watched him from the end of the bed, not moving a muscle.

My father's voice continued.

"Ever since I discovered the opening to Xona, there have been disturbing reactions, even at the highest level. It is as if we have not only opened a door into a whole other world, we have also opened a window onto peoples' hearts. We are beginning to understand the power of the spores. In the wrong hands, this power could be harnessed for self-interest and self-gain, leading to the destruction not only of Xona's rich life forms, but also the disruption of the delicate social harmony on our own planet. The future of both planets lies in the Arokah stone. Don't let it fall into the wrong …"

I could tell my father wanted to continue but the transmission seemed to end prematurely, as if he had been disturbed.

The Guardian powered the pad down and placed it back in the bedside drawer. He walked over to the stone tablet, and squatted in front of it, studying the symbols and shapes. He reached out his arms and took hold of the stone. Crouching, he grabbed hold of both corners, his golden medallion dangling loosely in front of the stone. Uttering a groan, he tried with all his strength to lift the tablet. His face went red with the exertion. The veins in his neck stuck out, causing his scar to fade for several heartbeats. After two more efforts, he knew he was defeated.

"Too heavy!"

The Guardian was muttering to himself.

Just then, something tickled my nose and I felt a sneeze forming. I thrust my hands over my face, pressing as tightly as I could, managing to mute the noise, but not silence it. The Guardian stood, looked around the room, and stared at the wardrobe.

He squinted, shaking his head, peering at the gaps in the door. He made a step towards me. Then another one. I was frozen now. Solid as the tablet in my room. Motionless. Terrified. Holding my breath. Cowering beneath my father's uniform, wishing that it was his strong arms, not his limp clothes covering me, holding me, protecting me from the man with the golden medallion, inches from the wardrobe door. I could see his hand reaching towards the handle, the black hair bristling on his knuckles. I was a heartbeat away from being discovered, maybe punished, worse even.

Then I heard the door hiss again.

The Guardian turned.

The crystals around his shoulders and in front of his forehead started to judder and turn this way and that.

It was Matron's voice and she wasn't happy. "I wasn't informed that you were making a visit to the student's quarters."

"I am the Guardian."

"I know who you are."

"Do you?" the Guardian asked. "Do you really know who I am?"

"These rooms are my responsibility," Matron said. "Don't visit again without informing me."

"The boy belongs to me," the Guardian said. "As does the stone."

"We shall see about that!" Matron cried.

The Guardian stood his ground for a good five seconds, glaring at Matron, who did not flinch or move an inch.

Then he stormed out of the room.

Matron waited before she followed. She turned to my qark, whose eyes had turned pitch black during the argument. She then turned to look at the patterns on the stone, shook her head, and left my cubicle, the door hissing behind her.

It took me ten minutes to climb down from my heightened state of anxiety, using my calming strategies, but when I had, I struggled out of the wardrobe, rubbed my legs to restore the blood flow, and then sat on my bed with Shin, whose eyes had turned from black to white.

I, meanwhile, pressed down on my palms, breathing in and out, desperate to calm my shattered nerves.

At that moment, I needed Meena. And at that moment, Meena came through the door.

She said sorry for interrupting my peace, but she didn't need to be. In a changing night sky, Meena was like a fixed and radiant sun. I really felt that I could trust her, even though I barely knew her, and her presence warmed and reassured me.

"Here," she said, holding out my golden Time Keeper. "You must have left it in your desk. I thought you should at least have it in your room. It's not wise to leave something this valuable lying about. Professor Kinzi told me to bring it to you."

I took the golden band, kicking myself that I'd been stupid enough to forget it and leave it at school, then wrapped it around my wrist. "I don't think I could be in any more trouble than I am right now," I said.

"What do you mean?"

I told her about the Guardian's intrusion and Matron's interruption of him. I shared everything they both said to each other, and all the while she looked more and more concerned.

"Even that drawer," I said, pointing. "My desk at school is probably safer. Honestly. Nothing's secure here. Anyone can walk in and out of here anytime they want. And they do!"

When I had finished, she sat on my bed and took Shin in her arms. Once again, he was behaving as a male, purring as she stroked him, smiling as she rubbed his belly.

"I've made up my mind," she said.

"What do you mean?"

"I've decided to help you. I know it's illegal. I know I will never get my license if I'm caught. But this is too important. It's more than a matter of life and death. Our very survival is at stake."

Shin's eyes began to glow bloodred.

"So, I'm going to fly you to Xona," she said.

The Guardian turned.
The crystals around his shoulders and in front of his forehead
started to judder and turn this way and that.

11
Red Smoke and Fiery Eyes

The next day, I couldn't stop pestering Meena, asking her during every break when we would be leaving and what we needed to do if we weren't to be found out. By the time the day's lessons ended, she had decided not to answer at all, except by smiling wearily and raising her hand in a gesture which after a while I took to mean, "Stop!"

After the final lesson, Meena and I stayed behind at the back of the classroom next to my desk.

"I see you've got the Time Keeper on," she said, looking at the golden strap on my wrist.

I nodded.

"Has it been giving you any trouble today?"

I shook my head.

"No burning sensations?"

"No."

I was not feeling talkative. The lack of clear directions about our secret mission had started to annoy me.

After the other 22 students had left, including Thunder Butt, who wanted to stay behind with us but was not allowed, the Professor came back into the classroom and beckoned to us.

"Meena, Khali, come this way please."

He led us to the front of the classroom and escorted us through a side door next to the raised platform where he had stood most of the day to teach us. We passed through another door and immediately entered what I can only describe as another world, or at least an ancient world. I had never seen anything like it, except in films of olden days when people had canvas pictures rather than monitors on their walls, and physical books on physical shelves rather than digital books in digital devices. The Professor's rooms were truly a portal into a bygone age.

"This is my study," he said. "Make yourselves at home."

The floorspace was large and covered in a frayed, woven carpet with four golden rimmed circles, with scaly, winged creatures in the middle of each. The edges of the rug were obscured by two burgundy leather armchairs on my left, and a sofa the same colour and material on my right. Like the Professor, they were old, yet comforting.

On both the left and right walls there were shelves in white peeling paint, I reckoned about ten on both sides, running along the length of the entire wall. Every shelf was crammed with books, many of them with old, gold covers, ornately rimmed and trimmed, like the antique volumes in the Library of Rantiki, in the heart of our capital city.

Directly ahead of us was the Professor's desk, which looked like it had been fashioned a long time ago from the Oaks of Dauron. Its dark brown wood was pitted and grooved like the Professor's skin. Its desktop was protected by a thin, rectangle of olive-green leather, attached to the wood by golden studs, now tarnished by black stains.

On the desk, there were more recent, less antique books lying clumsily on top of each other, like a tower about to collapse. I spotted some of the titles written on the spines.

Brain Mapping, by Rondo Kinzi.

The Hexagonal Array and Rhuboid Mobility, by Rondo Kinzi.

The End and the Means, by Arni Reikhl.

Feeding your Qark, by Fatso Macaroni.

The Professor sat down on a wooden chair that moved in the same direction as him. With one hand, he beckoned us to sit in the two armchairs, with the other he picked up a long, thin, curved implement with a tiny bowl at one end and what looked like a golden lip at the other. He took a small silver container, flicked a switch, and a flame appeared from the top. Raising the bowl, he lit whatever was in it and sat back in his chair, a puff of white smoke pouring out of his mouth in the direction of the ceiling.

"What's that?" I asked, as a haze of smoke began to form in the study. It had a strange, sweet and pleasant aroma.

"Tobacco smoke," the Professor said.

"I thought that was illegal," I said.

"It is, and rightly so, but it's the first and probably the only time I will ever light this thing. But you mark my words, don't you go copying me. If I ever hear that you've been smoking a pipe, I'll expel you from the Class of 24 before you can say 'but Professor'!"

Just then, his eyes lit up. He turned around and placed the puffing pipe on his desk. Some of the tobacco, still ignited, fell from the bowl onto a piece of paper, burning two small holes.

"Flip and bother!" he cried. "My late wife was right, may her dear soul rest in tranquillity. I am so clumsy. Always have been. Always will be. I'll have to clear up this mess later."

The Professor opened the front drawer of his desk. He produced a phial with a label on it: AS 321.

"Spores from one of your father's expeditions, Khali," he said as he tipped the contents from the glass container into the bowl of the pipe. "It might be interesting to see what happens when we combine them with the tobacco. Shall we give it a go?" He winked as he asked the question.

"I don't think that's a very good idea, Professor," Meena said, sighing as she looked at him lighting the bowl again.

"Oh, stuff and nonsense, Meena. You're much too cautious. What could possibly go wrong?"

He had an answer very quickly. The bowl suddenly turned into what I can only describe as a miniature cauldron. Smoke and fire billowed out of it. First it was white, then it was pink, then blue, then gold, finally red, all accompanied by tiny sparks and flashes.

At first, the smoke flowed out in thin and tiny streams, but as the colour turned to red, it poured out in huge gusts, creating an indoor storm cloud which filled the entire room.

Within several seconds, I could no longer see anyone, and my head started feeling light and happy. My eyes became hazy and bleary, as they tend to be between waking and sleeping.

The room now seemed to be moving and tipping, as if we were in a Space Ranger during an interstellar storm. Worse still, something seemed to be stirring at my feet, a large and heavy object, scaly and slimy, passing over first one foot, then the other. I looked down and to my horror, saw two golden eyes staring back at me. I hate eyes at the best of times, but these were horrible, and they were growing larger and larger until I realised with a rising sense of panic that the reason they were so big was because they were in front of me, just centimetres from my nose, staring right at me.

Just when I thought the creature was going to strike, another appeared from the side and pushed it out of the way, as if it wanted me all to itself. The first creature screeched as it reeled from the impact, then rallied and opened its ferocious jaws, bearing its long, jagged teeth, hissing at its assailant. Then a third appeared, ramming the second out of the way, before turning to face me. A long, slithering, saliva-moistened tongue, forked at the end, emerged from its mouth and started to lick my forehead, then my nose, my cheeks, my lips my chin, and finally my epiglottis.

I wanted to shout for help, but I was so scared I felt paralysed, unable to move a muscle, incapable of even basic speech.

Suddenly there were four of them.

The apex predators of our mythical past.

Like the ones on the Professor's rug.

Hissing.

Drawing closer.

Side by side.

Eyes of golden fire.

Teeth like daggers.

Their breath rotten and rancid.

Suddenly, in the twinkling of a burning eye, they vanished. All four of them. One moment they were in front of me, preparing to turn me into a meal, the next they were gone.

As I wiped my eyes, I saw the Professor. He had a glass of water in his hands and he was pouring it over the bowl of his pipe, extinguishing the smoke and the fire. He walked to a switch on the wall, pressed it, and all the odorous haze was sucked through a vent above us in the centre of the ceiling, out of the study and into the night sky, leaving the air in the room still and clean, as if nothing had happened.

"Perhaps that wasn't such a good idea," the Professor said.

"That should be the last of your pipe smoking," Meena said. "It's not just unhealthy. It's dangerous."

The Professor nodded. "Let's have some hot chocolate," he said after we had all calmed down. He left the room for a few minutes and then returned with a tray and three mugs, each one filled to the brim with a rich chocolatey drink and topped with what looked like small white and light blue clouds as sweet as anything I had ever tasted.

"You may think I was a little irresponsible with that rather unusual pipe experiment," the Professor said as he handed us our drinks. "However, I was making a point, a point I want you, Khali, to remember."

He sat down and took a sip of his hot chocolate.

"The truth is, anyone can use the spores for any purpose. They can use them for good and they can use them for evil. They can use them for selfish ends, or they can use them for the good of others."

The Professor wiped some stray marshmallow off his lips.

"For example, Khali, your father wanted to use the spores to make sure that there would be a cure for anyone suffering from the sickness that took your mother, so that no child should ever again have to go through what you have endured. Now that's what I call an unselfish use of the spores, one which all reasonable people would support."

The Professor put down his mug and sighed.

"But not everyone is like your father."

The Professor lifted a pad from his desk drawer and switched it on. He then swiped the glass several times and handed it to me.

"Do you know who this man is, Khali?"

The man's face was all scarred, his head covered in what looked like a black turban.

"I've never seen him before."

"He is one of the Ahketans," the Professor said.

I handed the pad back to the Professor.

"He wants the spores too, but his motives are neither good nor selfless. He wants to use them to medicate himself and to build a new and very dangerous power base on Kel."

"How do you know?" I asked.

"Your father told me. And…" he paused. "And we have a spy in the Class of 24 who is providing vital intelligence about him."

"Who?"

"All in good time, Khali. The important thing is to realise that this man and his followers pose a very clear and present danger, not only to the Class of 24, but to our planet and to our sister planet too. He plans to find what your father found, the purest form of energy from Xona, and to use this to rule over Kel and to plunder Xona."

Just then an old clock in the hallway beyond the study began to chime. The Professor let it finish before he said, "It's all a matter of time, Khali, and time is something we don't have. It's running out for Kel. It's running out fast. We need to act … now."

With that, the Professor pivoted on his chair and pointed to the wall above his desk. "Do you know what that is?"

There was a large, framed painting hanging there, almost as big as the space behind it. I had noticed it on entering the study but hadn't had time to mention it. It was a picture of a planet at night, a solitary object in an almost infinite expanse of dark space. There were swirls of white clouds over some parts, tiny lightning storms over others. The round surface was of varying colours, from snow white to rocky grey, from blue marble to an earthy brown colour. Deep blue patches covered most of the globe, oceans and great lakes. It looked beautiful and mysterious. Inviting too.

"Did your father ever mention going to this planet to you, Khali?" the Professor asked.

I shook my head.

"It's many light years away from here and would require your father's jump drive technology to get there, although he and I went there before you were born, using conventional engines. It took us six months. It's a planet that he and I named Endo Prime."

The Professor took his pad again and ran his fingers over the touch screen. He then passed it to me, telling me to swipe left and keep swiping until the slide show was finished. Nothing could have prepared me for what I saw. Landscapes of abundant life and striking colours. Oceans teeming with fish of all kinds and sizes. Forests with trees that seemed to reach for the sky. Birds with enormous wingspans that looked as if they could fly to the heavens and back. It took my breath away.

"We never landed there," the Professor said. "Your father and I sent out probes which took these shots. You are one of the very few people who knows about the planet and who's seen these pictures."

I finished looking at the pictures and put the pad down. A cloud of sadness passed over my heart as I realised that my father had been the first to see these images, along with the Professor. He had explored the far reaches of space to find a new home and he had found it here, on the planet he named "Endo Prime". I was so proud of him. And I missed him.

The Professor reached back towards his desk and picked up the long, curved pipe by its shank. It had now cooled down and stopped sending out tiny smoke signals, so he held it by the bowl.

"Do you know why I have this thing?"

I shook my head.

"It was owned by my ancestors and discovered by an archaeologist embedded in clay, in perfect condition, and in decent working order. It belonged to a member of my tribe, way back in the distant mists of time, before Kel became what it is now. The archaeologist estimates that it is probably over four thousand years old."

He put the pipe down on the desk.

"Sometimes you have to understand your history before you can live in your destiny," he said.

"What do you mean?"

The Professor leaned forward and propelled his chair towards me, until he was within an arm's length of my face.

"I know you don't enjoy this, but I want you to look at my face. The dark colour of my skin. The black blotches on my cheeks. And, if you can, the colour of my eyes."

I squinted, frowned and tilted my head, embarrassed at his closeness, yet intrigued by the puzzle.

"My hair was long and black once," he continued. "Just like your father's. Just like yours."

"Are we related, then?" I asked.

The Professor laughed. "We are all ultimately related, but no. Not closely. That would be too easy an answer to my question. Go deeper. Look further. Remember what I said, you have to appreciate your history if you're going to seize your destiny."

And then the lights in my head came on.

"We are from the same tribe," I cried. "The ancient ones, who inhabited the Great Plains, before the worm hole opened and the Ahketans arrived and occupied our land, our planet."

The Professor smiled. "And, what else?" he asked.

I searched my brain for an answer. Dad had once spoken about our people, how we had a special understanding of what it is like to be displaced and enslaved. He used to say that there were only few on Kel who really knew what it was like. He called us the Remnant.

The Remnant.

That was it!

"We are the last of them," I said. My voice was quiet, my eyes drawn away from the Professor to the fireplace. I hadn't noticed it when we first entered the study because the fire had almost gone out. But there were two coals in the hearth, both glowing, smouldering, dying.

"Like those embers," I said.

The Professor raised his bushy eyebrows. "A fitting yet sad comparison," he said. "And you are right. We are the Remnant, the last of our kind. When I go, there will only be you and a small handful of others left. You are to be their leader, Khali."

The Professor rose to his full height, pushed his chair back to the desk, and pointed to the picture of Endo Prime.

"So, you see, Khali. Your destiny is connected to your history. We are the last of a people who know what it is to be invaded and violated. One day, we may need to settle on Endo Prime. If so, we must not repeat the mistakes of the distant past."

I nodded, wondering if we would ever have to go there, and if we did, whether I really was as important as he said.

Before I had a chance to ask, the Professor turned back to face us.

"And now it's time to leave," he said. "I have somewhere to take you Khali, somewhere secret. Somewhere that's also connected to your destiny, and the destiny of Kel too."

12
The Temple of Tranquillity

The Professor turned towards the door at the far corner of the study. He was about to open it when he looked at the sofa, which was covered in papers and old maps. "Ah, there you are," he said.

He reached beneath the sheet and pulled something out from the recess beneath. I recognised it straightaway.

"A qark!" I said.

"This is Splink," the Professor said. "The oldest qark on Kel."

The qark did indeed look very old. Its hair, which was wispier and more matted than Shin's, was white and grey all over. It looked dishevelled and dusty, a bit like the Professor. And like the Professor, its eyes were obviously fading, because as soon as it was under his arm, the Professor took a tiny pair of spectacles, identical in all respects except size to his own, out of the breast pocket of his jacket and placed them on his qark's twitching nose. As soon as they were perched there, Splink started to look at me. Then Meena. Then me. Finally, it turned its head sideways towards the Professor and its eyes turned a bright white colour.

"These two are indeed good and kind, Splink," he said. "Your powers have not yet waned, your discernment is still strong."

The qark seemed to smile before the Professor put it back into its hiding place beneath the map. He withdrew from his pocket a long chew, which I knew was a Splodge – one of the latest and most popular treats on our planet – and put it close to Splink's nose. There was a shuffling sound, followed by a snuffling noise, and then it was gone.

And so were we.

The door from the study led outside to a landing pad where a silver transporter with red wingtips was waiting for us. The Professor beckoned us to follow him up the ramp at the rear of the craft and into three of the four seats behind the pilot. The transporter's cargo door closed and its engines sprang into life. Within five seconds, we were airborne above the city, looking down on the square shapes of the buildings, some tall, others squat, a few more somewhere between the two.

"You were right," the Professor said to me. "Our architecture needs upgrading. Hexagons are far more efficient. Not to mention beautiful. We'll get you to do some concept drawings for the new accommodation blocks I'm planning at our secret location."

Seventeen minutes later, the transporter began to decelerate and then descend. The light of the late afternoon sun was beginning to fade. I had to stir myself from an almost trance-like state, born from gazing at the lights that had been coming on in the buildings in the suburbs, then the fewer pinpricks of light that had punctuated the fertile, rural plains reaching towards the very circumference of the great dome.

"We're here," the Professor said.

"What is this place?" I asked.

"Wait and see," Meena replied. "I think you'll be impressed. You're in for quite a surprise."

The Transporter hovered above a forest of very high trees before homing in on what looked like a wide and open square space, then alighting on a landing pad in the middle of what looked to me like a vast, paved courtyard. Surrounding this yard, on three sides, there were clumps of smaller trees, with empty benches beside jade green ponds covered in pink and white lotus flowers. Beyond these there were pagodas and grottoes which ran right up to a tall wall enclosing the entire area, at the edge of the dense forest.

As we left the ramp and walked to the front of the Transporter, I could see the shape of a strange building standing about four hundred paces ahead. From above, it had been invisible, as if its colours and shape had been designed to blend in with the wooded surroundings. Up close, I could see that it was a single storey building with two eaves and two sloping roofs, the highest of which had a ridge with two carved herons at each end. The nearer we got to it, the richer the aromas that assaulted our nostrils. The entire area was filled with a strong fragrance from the waxy fruit of bayberry bushes, mixed with the sweet scent from the flowers of the small Osmanthus trees.

"The Temple of Xona," the Professor said, heading towards the deep blue building, which now seemed to be shrouded with mist from the trees. "Also known as the Temple of Tranquillity."

"I didn't know this had been built," I said.

"It's a secret," the Professor said.

We reached the end of the path and crossed a small bridge. Skirting around a fountain with crystal-clear running water, we climbed a set of low steps and then stopped at the entrance to the Temple. The two golden doors moved outwards towards us. When they had fully opened, the Professor pointed to an inscription on a

Lagentum plaque on the wall. "Pause upon this threshold and devote yourself to peace."

"Peace be to Kel, and peace be to our Great Sister," the Professor muttered as we stepped into a hall. Even in the half-light I could see that its walls were filled with painted carvings of the fire-breathing predators I had seen in the Professor's study, believed by our ancient ancestors to be the inhabitants and the stokers of Kel's volcanoes.

We entered a side room and sat on a mat on the stone floor, cut from the rocks of our planet.

"Time for refreshments," the Professor said, walking to an open fireplace and placing a pot over the flames crackling in the hearth. While the liquid was coming to a boil, he thrust some toasting forks between the burning coals and the whistling pot. Within minutes, there was a low-level table in front of Meena and me, with hot apple punch and jam-filled truffins on it, the ones the Professor had promised.

"It's so quiet here," I said, after drinking some of the warm sweet juice. The liquid was truly sensational; it satisfied all my senses all at once, making my tongue tingle and my eyes drowsy.

"In this place, our words are few," the Professor said. "There is too much talk and too much noise in the world. Here, we believe in closing our mouths and opening our ears, choosing to listen to the birds calling out to the dawn, and the wolves greeting the dusk." The Professor shuffled his old haunches to get more comfortable. "Beside which," he added, "some of our number find that loud or sudden noises are very painful."

I took a bite out of my jam-centred truffin. Its soft pastry and strong cocoa covered my tongue and filled my mouth. Within seconds, all the uncertainty and anxiety of the journey had gone.

"Do you always sit on the floor?" I asked the Professor.

"The lower you go, the higher you fly," he replied.

I put down my cup and lay my body, face down, on the cold stone floor, my arms stretched out as far as they would go, my fingertips pressing down on the ground.

"That's good," the Professor said. "Very good."

I stayed there for 60 seconds, all of which I counted in my head, then sat back in my place and finished my apple punch, savouring the aroma of the spices in my nostrils.

I drank every drop.

"That's good too," the Professor said. "Nothing wasted."

He slowly rose to his feet and then ushered us to follow him back into the hall. We passed through some ornate doors into a great chamber, with what looked like a stone table on a dais at the far end, under a canopy of dragons' wings carved in gold. The table was bare, but when we drew near, I could see that it had a small trench carved in the very centre. It looked like a port in which something was supposed to dock.

"What's that for?" I asked, pointing to the groove.

"I think you know the answer already," the Professor replied.

Then Meena took over. "Khali," she said in a soft and reverent voice. "This is the Temple of Xona. Only those who honour the Great Sister are allowed here, only those whom the Professor deems have good and loyal hearts, which is why you're here."

"And all the others," the Professor added.

"What others?"

No sooner had the words come out of my mouth, I began to be aware of shapes in the shadows around the walls of the chamber. There was movement on the peripheries of the room. I could sense it. People, coming out of the darkness, walking towards the centre of the room, forming one long line, facing the stone table, their heads bowed.

As my eyes adjusted to the dim lighting, I realised I couldn't make out any of them. They were all wearing robes with hoods that covered the back and sides of their heads.

The Professor came and stood at my side as I faced the phalanx of strangers. "These people are all committed to two great causes. The enhancement of life on Kel, and the protection of life on Xona. We are not prepared to have one at the expense of the other. That would be a violation of the laws of harmony and balance. No, we believe in the best of both worlds and the best for both worlds."

As he uttered that final remark, I turned to smile at Meena, remembering the same words that she had uttered from her lips in the classroom just the day before. But she had left the stone table while the Professor had been talking to me, and a new figure had joined the row in front of me, dressed in white as all the rest, with a cowl concealing their identity.

"Khali," the Professor said, turning towards the altar, pulling me on my sleeve to face it too. "I need to tell you something. Something that may come as a surprise to you."

I held my breath.

"Your father designed this stone table and placed it on this dais, just days before he disappeared on Xona."

"I … I … didn't know," I said.

"He was preparing everything, including you."

Then it hit me.

The groove in the stone table behind me was the same size and shape as the base of the Arokah stone in my bedroom back at the Beacon. Dad had created this small trench as a port in which to dock the tablet. This Temple was the place where he wanted it to be kept. This building, in my head, was the House of the Stone.

"He dreamed of such a place," the Professor said. "And he saw a great light pouring from this stone table. A great energy that could generate all that we will need to sustain life in this hidden location, all that we would need to create what we need to protect ourselves and prepare for the future, even if that future is away from Xona, on Endo Prime."

The Professor took me by the arm.

"Khali," he said. "When you have placed the tablet on the table, the light that flows from it will attract the darkness as much as it will dispel it. That is why we have to get ready. Everyone must get ready. Only the strong can guard this light. Only the wise can use it well."

Then he turned to me, looking into my eyes. I wanted to look away, but I couldn't. It was as if his pupils were like planets, pulling me into their orbit, drawing me into their atmosphere.

"Do you want to become a gatekeeper in this secret Temple and a guardian of the sacred stone?"

I nodded.

"Say it," the Professor said.

"I do."

"Do you want to protect the life and light of Xona from all those who would abuse its power?"

"Yes," I replied.

"Do you accept the destiny passed onto you by your father, to walk in the light and to stand against the darkness?"

"I accept it."

"Then turn and face the other guardians."

I looked at the row of hooded people.

"How many are there?" the Professor asked.

I counted. "Twenty-three."

Then it hit me, as one by one, they began to remove their hoods, revealing their faces. And one by one, I recognised them. Meena. Demorah. Even Thunder Butt was there. I was staring open-mouthed at all the other members of the Class of 24.

"Welcome to the Guardians of the Temple," the Professor said. "Now take this and put it on."

I clothed myself in the same hooded gown that the others had been wearing. Then the Professor led me into the centre of a large, ornate circle carved in the stone floor.

The Class of 24 began to form around me.

"Do you promise to keep this place a secret from all others?" the Professor asked.

"I do," I replied.

"And do you promise to bring the stone tablet that your father made to the table, where you will guard it?"

"I do."

"And do you promise to be one with your fellow Guardians, even as they are one with you?"

"I do."

"Then join them."

Meena stepped to one side to create a gap.

"Now you are complete," the Professor said.

It was only as I looked around me that I realised that the Guardians, now 24 including me, had formed a hexagon, with the Professor in the centre.

"And now you are ready," the Professor said. "Gather your things and leave immediately."

13
Spying on the Enemy

After saying goodbye to the others at the launch pad, and returning on the Ranger to the Beacon, my urgency was fuelled by my new sense of destiny. I knew what I was supposed to do, and I knew that I was not alone. There was Meena. There was the Professor. And there were the 23 other members of my class. I was one of the Guardians now.

On the way back from the Temple, the Professor had sat next to me and Meena on the Transporter. "I have a secret to share with you, a secret that you can share with no one," he said.

I half smiled inside. I was beginning to enjoy being the keeper of secrets.

"The cannon I have designed…"

I nodded.

"Well, it won't work. I mean, it *can't* work. It won't work, because I've ensured there's a flaw in the casing of the shells. It *can't* work because we, the Guardians, must not allow Xona's delicate ecosystem to be ruined by a selfish desire for the spores."

"How do we know the cannon will be used at all?" I asked.

"The Ahketans decide tomorrow," the Professor answered with a frown. "I am expecting them to vote for the weapon to be used."

Meena, who had been sitting the other side of the Professor, interrupted. "Why are you so convinced, Professor?"

"I have already told you that there is one among the Ahketans intent on exploiting Xona's rich resources for his own ends, and who has been, let's say, stirring up dissent."

There were seven Ahketans in all, and they were voted into their positions of great power by our Parliament. Since ancient times, their main role had been to act as Global Justices, establishing our laws, judging complicated cases where old laws did not seem to apply, and where new laws needed to be formed. In more recent centuries, their function had become less judicial and more governmental. Our Parliament had given them more and more authority to provide leadership and wisdom on a wide range of issues – energy, population control, land development, respect for minorities, and the careful use of natural resources on our planet. Never in our history had they been divided on the decisions they had to make.

Until now.

Meena escorted me back to her room at the Beacon. It was in a part of the building which I hadn't been allowed to visit. Inhabited by the seniors – those who were in their final year at the Academy – it was strictly out of bounds to those as young as me. They had way more freedom than us juniors. Their rooms were much more spacious, with bedrooms separated from their recreational and work areas. Even better, each room had an exit that led straight out onto a thin long stretch of paving that acted as a landing pad for their hover scooters. Every senior had one to themselves, and they were allowed anywhere in the Academy until curfew, just before midnight.

I was jealous, and glad that there was no qark in her quarters to show off its bright green eyes. But then qarks were for newbies. And for old people who live on their own and like a bit of company.

Like the Professor.

Meena led me into her recreational chamber, a room with a large screen on the wall, and three comfortable chairs. As I sat down next to a table, I saw a photograph of a woman I took to be her mother. She was beautiful, like Meena. The same auburn hair, pale face, freckled forehead and wide, genuine smile. The likeness was unmistakable.

"She was the most amazing woman I've ever met," Meena said as she re-entered the room with some food. "No woman has ever replaced her. No woman ever could. She was one of a kind."

"Not even Matron?" I asked.

"Especially not Matron, darlink." Meena chuckled.

I wasn't laughing though. I was thinking about Meena. I couldn't believe that her father had done the things he did to her. How was such darkness even possible on our world?

"Can I ask you something?" I said.

"Of course."

"Who is the person the Professor was talking about, the Ahketan who's causing all the trouble?"

Meena sat down. "His name is Reikhl," she said. "He's the newest and the youngest of the Ahketans, although he looks by far the oldest."

Meena noted my confused expression. The youngest who looks the oldest. That was not logical, at least on the surface of it. It was a description demanding an explanation.

"Very few people know his story," Meena continued. "The Professor told me one day after school. Reikhl is really only 25 years old, but he looks very much older because he has…"

"Yes?" I said. Meena had paused.

"He has White Line."

I frowned. White Line was a very rare disease on our planet, and greatly feared. It was caused by a rare, intracellular bacterium and was incurable. Its symptoms were dreadful. Gradual whitening of the flesh. Permanent nerve damage. A growing numbness and inability to feel pain in the infected areas, some of which took on the appearance of solid rock. Worse of all, the highly pigmented skin lesions eventually falling off altogether. Fingers. Toes. Entire limbs. All leading to a slow and painful death.

"The story goes that he was sent by the other Ahketans to a remote village around the Arian Falls. His task was to devise a project of self-empowerment for the people, to bring them out of poverty and disease. Being the youngest of their group, they considered him to be the best placed to undertake such an arduous mission."

Meena leaned forward. "When he got there, he found that those left alive were riddled with White Line. Reikhl only realised when it was too late. By then he had been infected. When he returned, he was placed in quarantine. Since then he has lived in isolation on a high outpost, served by droids, talking and adjudicating with the other Ahketans only by video link."

"So that's why he looks so old," I said.

Meena didn't answer. She took a remote device out of the arm of her chair and pointed it towards the screen on the wall in front of us. Within two seconds, Meena had located and downloaded a file.

"This is a secret film taken by one of us. No one outside the Class of 24 has seen it."

The images were taken from a camera hidden within some sculptured metal fronds outside a solitary apartment on a raised and remote eerie, like the mountain nest of a great bird of prey. Whoever was shooting the film was being careful not to be seen. As they trained the camera on the building, they zoomed in on the only window visible. This was on the side looking out across the city, so only a small portion of the glass was visible. Just enough, however, to make out a figure standing in the darkness, his silhouette highlighted against the dying sun. There was only dim lighting in the room, so the camera operator switched to night vision mode, bathing the target in a green hue.

I could see the person, or the creature, now. He was tall. Dressed entirely in what looked like a black uniform with a glossy, silky sheen to it, like the colour of the night. On his head, he wore a mask that covered his face and neck. This mask looked as if it was carved from a precious metal. It had a sharp beak at the front, with two golden eyes just above and behind, and long black feathers protruding from the top and the back, making the man resemble one of the savage hunter ravens of Goldor.

As the Time Keeper on my wrist began to grow warm, it struck me; I was staring at the shadow that had come to my room.

The filming continued for about thirty seconds until the man seemed to be experiencing some difficulties. He reached up to his head as if in pain. Something seemed to be wrong. He shouted to someone. An android appeared from the shadows and stood beside him. It helped the man remove his head dress, taking great care not to cause any distress, and then placed the birdlike object on a table next to his master.

My Time Keeper was hot now.

At first, all I could make out was the man's hair. White, wavy hair. Lots of it. Unwashed. Unkempt. Tangled. Brushed upwards and backwards, as if he'd been standing for a long time in a wind tunnel.

Then I saw his face. He looked at least sixty years old. His skin was pale from his neck to his forehead, almost blanched in the bright green hue of the night vision camera. More striking still were the marks all over his face, like grooves cut in stone, and the craggy flesh that once was soft tissue. His forehead looked like an ancient rock formation and the sad eyes beneath it looked like dying planets. There were papules all over his cheeks and his chin, from which the remnants of a goatee beard – once black and groomed – hung like the drooping branches of a dying tree.

I felt compassion for him.

"If you look, Khali, you'll see that Reikhl almost senses someone watching him, like a wild animal being tracked in a hunt. See how he turns to where the camera is, then barks a command to the droid."

I saw it. The look of anger on the man's face. The sudden drawing down of the automatic blinds, like the closing of the eyelids on a corpse. The interior of the apartment now invisible. The building lifeless. Lightless. Shrouded in the last glow before dusk.

"Who took those pictures?" I asked, taking off my Time Keeper, which had become quite uncomfortable.

"He's outside," Meena said, pressing the touch-sensitive screen of her watch, then typing something. "They were taken just two nights ago, after the Professor's speech in Parliament. The person who did it was incredibly brave and extraordinarily resourceful. In fact, there's only one person I know who could have done this."

Just then, the door outside in the hall hissed, and then the one into the recreation chamber.

Across the threshold stepped the one person I was least expecting to qualify as courageous and resourceful. The one person I would never have imagined capable of such a daring feat of espionage.

It was Thunder Butt.

And he was smiling.

"You'll have to excuse me," he said with a chuckle, his cheeks flushed from running. "I'm a bit windy tonight."

"You're always a bit windy," Meena said, with more than a hint of weariness, some of which might have been put on.

"Was it really you?" I asked.

"Yes, Khali. Just because I'm large, doesn't mean I can't be useful."

"I'm sorry, Thunder Butt," I said. "I didn't mean anything."

He nodded and smiled.

"Thunder Butt went back again last night," Meena said. "He's seen and heard more."

"I did," he said. "I watched a droid go to the entrance of Reikhl's apartment. Everything is voice activated there, so I used my Impersonator device to mimic the droid's way of speaking. Then, when it was way after curfew and everything was quiet, I went up to the voice recognition panel and imitated the droid. It worked. I was in!"

"That's brave," I said. "You could have caught the disease."

"He knows what to do to avoid that," Meena said.

"I slithered like a snake, a very fat snake," Thunder Butt patted his belly with a proud smile, "and made my way into a dark room. It was very scary, and I had to squeeze my butt cheeks really tight together to stop myself from waking the whole place up. But I managed. Somehow. And what I saw there, well, it really was scary."

"Even I haven't heard this part yet," Meena said.

"The room was empty except for one thing, right in the centre. A long box, like a coffin. With strange sounds, hissing sounds, like steam being discharged, coming from openings in both sides of the inside of the box, from the top to the bottom. It smelt like wet rocks."

Meena and I didn't move a muscle. I was afraid and already feeling the first hints of freezing. But I resisted the temptation and listened to the end of the story, my curiosity defeating my anxiety.

"The box was made of Lagentum and Reikhl was lying in it, in a kind of trance. His mask was off, his gown off, and he was naked. I saw everything, including…" Thunder Butt sneered. "Including his … privates."

"Yuk!" I cried.

"No time for that," Meena said. "What happened next?"

"Well, while he was in this trance, his body twitched every time the steam was released. And each time the tiny clouds touched his skin, the patches seem to decrease a little in size, and the whiteness seem to fade a little too, leaving those areas soft and clear. As I watched, his whole appearance changed. He went from being an old man to a young man."

Meena gasped.

"But it was a strange kind of young," Thunder Butt continued. "Like he was not quite one of us, his skin a pale and ghostly blue, his eyes a darker, deeper blue. Handsome almost. But scary handsome."

"Reikhl is using the spores to rejuvenate his skin tissue," I said. "No wonder he is so eager to blast holes in Xona's membrane. He wants access to the undiluted energy there. He thinks it can change him permanently, so he doesn't have to keep doing this every night."

"Precisely," Meena said. "The spores he's somehow acquired for himself are not strong enough to cure his disease altogether. He believes that the energy on Xona itself is far more powerful."

"He's right," I said.

"How do you know?" Thunder Butt asked.

"You can trust him," Meena said to me.

So, I told my story, as I had to Meena.

"You've been to Xona?" Thunder Butt cried.

I nodded.

"Is it different there, the energy?"

"My dad told me that the energy on Xona is found in three states," I answered. "The crystalized membrane, the spore clouds, and the power source on the planet. Reikhl knows that the spores he currently possesses are not the most powerful form of this energy."

Thunder Butt spoke, his voice lowered. "Time is short. The Professor estimates that there are just two days left before the opening will become too small for a runabout to pass through it. And he has no intention of letting Reikhl and his supporters blast holes in the membrane to create new openings."

"What are you saying?" I asked.

"I'm saying that Reikhl may suspect that there isn't much time before the one existing hole closes. I believe he may well attempt a last, desperate dash to Xona to steal what he can of the planet's energy."

"But he's isolated and forbidden to travel anywhere beyond his remote outpost," I said.

"He has a runabout docked the far side of his apartment, invisible from public view. I saw it before I left last night. It has the picture of a hunter raven on the side of the cockpit. It's definitely Reikhl's and I suspect it's the first in a fleet he's building."

"But he can't fly it himself," Meena said.

"There was a pilot droid sitting in the cockpit, as if he was waiting for take-off," Thunder Butt replied. "I don't know how we're going to stop him, but we've got to."

"I agree," Meena said. "There are only two people I trust to look after the power of Xona, should the Great Sister choose to trust us with it, and that is the Professor and you, Khali. He wants the best for both worlds, Xona's and ours, and he will never, ever destroy another planet in order to promote his own interests. I trust him with my life."

"Then I must tell him what I've seen," Thunder Butt said.

"And I want to help," Khali said. "Everything you've said confirms that I have to go back to Xona. We must do something, *soon!*"

It was Thunder Butt who spoke next. "You're right," he said. "We need to go tomorrow night."

"*We?*" I said.

"Yes," Thunder Butt replied. "I'm coming too."

More striking still were the marks all over his face, like grooves cut in stone, and the craggy flesh that once was soft tissue. His forehead looked like an ancient rock for-mation and the sad eyes beneath it looked like dying planets.

14
Bees Wax and Bugs

I suppose everybody has their own way of preparing for a dangerous mission; mine was to do my hair.

It was the morning after I had seen the secret film of Reikhl, taken by Thunder Butt, and I was sitting in front of the mirror on the desk in my room. I had taken all my mother's hair products and implements out of her flowery bag in my closet and turned my desk into a dressing table. I had just washed my hair in the boys' showers down the corridor and dried it in my room.

That day was not just our one day off each week from school. It was also our National Holiday, when we commemorate the exodus of the last remaining survivors from our original planet. Almost a millennium ago, a fleet of Ahketans had passed through a wormhole and landed on Kel, making it their new home.

No one worked today. The Beacon was unusually quiet. The corridor outside my room had been empty. I had climbed out of bed early, waking with Shin when the first light of the day penetrated the tiny gaps in my blinds. Everyone was sleeping late in preparation for the parties that would follow. Everyone except me, that is. And

Meena, who arrived in my room just before I finished doing my hair the way I wanted it.

"This is a good night for it," she whispered as she sat on my bed, straightening and parting Shin's hair with one of my mother's brushes. Shin seemed to have suspended his normal, empathic response mechanisms. Its whole body had gone into some sort of super-relaxed state. Its eyes, which were squinting with pleasure, were closing so tightly that I couldn't see what colour they were. Sitting on Meena's lap, it – no, "he" – purred and whined with pleasure, teetering on the edge of bliss.

"Everyone will be home with their families and neighbours," she said. "People won't be as watchful as usual, and the number of sentinels on duty at the space dock will be very small. They will be automated rather than human. While they won't be partying, everyone else will."

"Not everyone," I said.

I could see from her reflection in my mirror that Meena wanted an explanation, so I provided one.

"My mother was white-skinned, yes, but my father had the dark toned features of a native Kelan, so I don't feel the same."

Meena didn't need me to explain. When the fleet of surviving Ahketans had come through the wormhole, they had landed on the Great Plains of Seskebar, where my father's, and the Professor's, ancestors lived, working the land, living in harmony with each other and the world. They had been one great tribe, created out of many smaller tribes, brought together by a shared vision for breaking down dividing walls and establishing one common family whose unity would be their strength. All that was lost when the fleet arrived. My father's ancestors stood no chance against the greater technology of the visitors, whose weapons were far more advanced. Even their oneness couldn't save them from being displaced or compelled to work for their new masters.

"Dad always found it difficult," I said. "Even though there has been much healing, it still hurt him to think of it. Today, of course, our population is made up of many different looking human beings, all celebrated for their uniqueness. But it wasn't like that at the beginning."

Meena nodded. Shin's eyes opened for a second and glowed with a grey hue, the colour of sadness.

"Did your Mum have wavy hair?" Meena asked.

I nodded.

Meena stepped away from the bed and stood behind me.

"I'm guessing you have to work hard at keeping yours straight," she said, taking the brush from the dressing table. "Do you mind?" she asked before starting to use it.

I shook my head.

As she started to brush, she took a strand of my hair in her hands and inspected it. "It's funny," she said. "When I first saw you, I thought your hair was jet black. But now, this close, I can see dark brown too."

"That's Mum," I said. "It's the same deal with my eyes. Everyone thinks they're black, but they have a tint of dark reddish brown. I have a bit of both my parents in my hair, my eyes, my skin colour."

I leaned forward towards the mirror and pressed my finger against my tanned cheeks. "Do you see the whiteness when I press?"

Meena nodded.

"My skin isn't as dark as my father's, although I do have his big black freckles under both my eyes. I'm such a mixture." I tilted my head sideways. "Do you see my jawline? It's pronounced, like Dad's. But I don't have his high, prominent cheekbones."

"You really are a mixture," Meena said, taking my hair and brushing it. Then, without warning, she started giggling.

"What is it?"

"Your ears," she said. "They are so cute."

I took the brush from her hands and covered my ears.

"One's flat," I said, "like Dad's. The other is round, like Mum's. I keep my hair this long so no one will see."

Meena stopped giggling and apologised.

"It's okay," I said. "It's mainly because I love symmetry that I don't like people seeing them."

"You have some really cool, old-fashioned hair products," she said, changing the subject. "What's this one, here?"

"Beeswax," I said, digging two fingers into the sticky, yellow substance. "It's from my father's beehive. Dad used to make some into hair gel for Mum. The rest he made into candles, which he lit on their wedding anniversary. They would have dinner while the candles burned."

"They must have really loved each other," Meena said.

I warmed the beeswax in my hands, rubbing it in my palms, then applied it to the unruly hair on the top of my head, creating a wavier effect on my scalp, while the straight hair from the sides fell over my ears as far as the nape of my neck and the tops of my shoulders.

"You look good," Meena said. "You should do this more often."

"No," I said. "I only take this amount of time on special occasions, like the anniversary of my mum's death. Most kids do things with their hair to feel different. I do it because these are all Mum's things. I don't want them ever to run out."

I looked in the mirror. I could almost see her looking back, in the white shades on my face and the dark brown tints in my eyes and hair. I touched the lobe of my rounded right ear, the one shaped after the fashion of my mother's, and I felt the tears begin to form. I think I would have surrendered to them had it not been for the hiss of the door.

I turned to see Thunder Butt, a finger over his lips, another gadget of some sort in his free hand. It had an antenna protruding from the top, and a red light flashing on it.

Shin sat on his haunches and looked at our visitor, his eyes radiating with a pink colour. Pink means playful. Also, immature. I wasn't sure which it was until five seconds later.

Thunder Butt lifted the device and pointed it at every part of the room. From time to time the red light would flash even faster, before subsiding again to its original rate. He smiled, then giggled.

I was about to ask him what he thought he was doing, when he placed his finger over my lips. I could smell honey. He had eaten pancakes for breakfast. Knowing Thunder Butt, a lot of them.

As Meena thrust out her hands, as if to ask him what he was up to, Thunder Butt took my mother's hair dryer and switched it on. The room was filled with its loud whirring as he pointed at the closet door. Five seconds later, we were all three crammed inside with only the flashing red light from the gadget to provide any relief from the darkness.

"We will have to whisper," he said, as the hairdryer continued to whir like the thrusters on my father's Ranger. "Rock Face has ears and eyes everywhere, including in your room, Khali."

"Rock Face?" I said.

"That's my name for Reikhl. Didn't you see his cheeks and his forehead on my film? His skin reminds me of the crags and scars of the limestone rock at Danda's Cove. They're called 'grykes'. Rock Face sounds better than Gryke Face, don't you think?"

I nodded. It really did.

"What's going on?" Meena asked, her voice lowered.

"It's all planned," Thunder Butt whispered. "We will leave from the Professor's room tonight. He's given us permission to use his vessel. I have a few tricks up my sleeve for leaving undetected."

Thunder Butt then looked at me. "How are you feeling, Khali?"

"What do you mean?"

"About exploring the cave on Xona."

"I'm excited about finding the light."

"That's not what he meant," Meena interjected. I must have looked confused, because she added, "About possibly finding your dad's…" She paused for a second. "Your dad's remains."

That was a fair question. The previous night I had passed in and out of sleep, dreaming of finding my father's body. In one of them, his face was swollen, and his eyes looked as if they were about to pop out of his head as he stared vacant and lifeless through the glass of his visor. I had woken up from that image in a sweat. Only Shin's intervention had brought me down from my high and chilling state of dread.

"I guess I need some answers now," I said, as I continued to think of my father's eyes.

Meena put her hand on my arm. We were all quiet for a few seconds, with the hair dryer still blowing in the background.

"I'll go with you into the cave," Thunder Butt said. "We don't want you to be on your own, do we Meena?"

Just then, my nostrils were overwhelmed by a horrible smell. "What's that?" I asked.

It reminded me of the food waste at the end of our meals in the canteens, only a hundred times worse.

"I'm nervous!" Thunder Butt protested.

"Oh, Thunder Butt!" Meena cried out in a muted voice. "You're really vile sometimes."

Meena and I couldn't stand it any longer. Thunder Butt was obviously fine about remaining within the atmosphere of his foul-smelling farts, but we were most certainly not. We broke out of the closet gasping and groaning, coughing out the contaminated air. As we did, Shin, who was sitting on the edge of my bed, sensed the smell too and fell onto the floor, trying to cover his nose with his tiny front paws.

Thunder Butt joined us a few seconds later, his face as red as the flashing button on his bug detector. Putting his finger to his thick lips again, he pointed to the tablet standing against the wall next to the door.

"Is that the stone?" he whispered.

I nodded.

"And you're bringing it tonight?"

I nodded again.

Thunder Butt looked a little confused. He could see that it was very heavy, so he bent down to try and lift it. He puffed out his flushed cheeks several times. He couldn't move it at all.

"How?" he mouthed.

I leaned down and took hold of the top of the stone in one hand. I lifted it without any effort.

"It's the effect of the spores," I whispered.

Meena stepped over to the hair dryer and switched it off. The room fell quiet again.

"Cool waves," Thunder Butt said to me, looking at my head.

"Thanks."

"Did you use this stuff?" he asked, picking up the tin of beeswax.

I was about to answer when the door hissed again.

"Hello darlinks," Matron said. She was a little out of breath, as if she had been running. "What little plots are you hatching?"

We shook our heads as if to say, "Nothing."

"I hope you're going to stay out of the kitchens today, Loois," she added, a stern frown on her forehead.

The previous morning, the canteen droids had sprinkled salt instead of sugar on everybody's porridge. Thunder Butt, who never seemed to sleep, had changed the containers in the early hours of the morning, resulting in a lot of sour faces from the students, and yet another detention for him.

"Trust me, Matron," Thunder Butt replied. "I'm not going anywhere near the kitchens today, or this evening."

"Well, whatever it is you're doing, make sure it's within the school and that you don't break the rules. No mischief. No nonsense. Be a good boy and don't lead your peers astray."

"Would I ever?" Thunder Butt said.

"Yes, I'm sure you would," she replied. "And I'm equally sure you're up to no good. I'm going to ask you again. What is it?"

Thunder Butt lifted the tin in his hands, opened it, and before Khali could stop him filching some of his mother's precious wax, he thrust a big finger into the yellow and clay-like substance. He sniffed the end of it, then ran it through his hair and closed the tin again. Without even a hint of trepidation, he looked Matron in the eye.

"None of your beeswax," he said, before leaving the room.

15
The Shrinking Portal

That night, as parties sprung to life across our planet, I put on the costume Meena had brought that morning. All three of us had decided to dress as qarks, not only because we thought it would be fun, but also it had become something of a tradition, due to the many different colours and shapes possessed by these creatures. Thousands of people would be clothed the same way, and we would therefore be able to mingle unnoticed among the crowds as we made our way to the Professor's launchpad.

When I had put on my costume, which was remarkably light considering how much multi-coloured hair there was hanging from it, Shin went wild with joy. Its master had become a larger version of itself and it was rolling over on its back, yelping with glee and chirruping with joy. I laughed and bent down to stroke it, then rolled over just as it was rolling over, snuggling into its soft fur, imitating its sounds.

"Time for me to go," I said in a determined voice after a few more attempts at imitating my qark.

I lifted the Arokah stone and placed it within a thin backpack, which I covered with the same material as my costume. I hauled it over my shoulders, checking in the mirror to see if it was visible. It was not.

I put on the golden Time Keeper, which had been lying on my bedside table since the previous night and made for the door. "See you later, Shin," I whispered as I left my room and made my way along the empty corridor and out of the front doors of the Beacon.

There were thousands of people along the route to the Space Academy Headquarters, all dressed in costumes, many of them qarks as Meena had anticipated. Some of them rubbed themselves against me, but I moved on quickly, not appreciating the uninvited contact, not appreciating it at all. Perhaps I was a little anxious, apprehensive about the mission ahead, still dreading what I might or might not find of my father. My dislike of strangers' hugs, a symptom of my Rhuba, was therefore intensified. I just wanted to walk alone, so it was a great relief when I saw the avenue of trees leading to the tall and familiar building, the Class of 24 at its summit. I had reached my goal, and I had reached it undetected, as far as I could tell.

I passed through the foyer, wiping a bead of sweat from my brow. The heat generated and the qark outfit, were beginning to take their toll. I was grateful for the wafts of wet air from the water sculptures on my way; it was tempting to jump under the jet of cool water from the fountain near the elevator.

I began to ascend in the lift. While there had been people blowing toy trumpets and pulling party poppers on the ground floor, I found the top of the building deserted. I walked through my empty classroom to the door at the far end, leading to the Professor's private quarters.

"Welcome, Khali," he said as I entered his study. It was as untidy as the last time I'd seen it. "You have heard the news, I presume. Parliament has voted to blast holes in the crystal membrane."

"No," I said.

"May I have a look at it?" the Professor asked, pointing to the tablet as I removed it from the backpack.

I nodded.

"You can put your flying uniforms on now," he said, kneeling to examine the Lagentum plate and its strange symbols. "Remarkable," he said. "Quite remarkable."

Using a magnifying glass, the Professor began to inspect it with intense focus. As he did, I winced as I saw one of his eyes enlarged by the glass. He reminded me of the big stone fish in the foyer.

"Hmm," he muttered as he continued to look. "It is a most ingenious and unusual puzzle. It is made up of what you might call pieces, except these pieces are not separated physically. I assume they move telekinetically."

I nodded. "Meena and I think that the stone is connected with the energy of Xona, so I'm bringing it with us."

"Very good," he said. "Very good."

The Professor didn't have time to ask any more questions. Meena and Thunder Butt walked in, dressed as qarks. Thunder Butt's costume was bigger and hairier than Meena's. He looked ginormous.

"Put on your flight uniforms," the Professor said.

"Is Meena allowed to be our pilot?" I asked.

"She has my permission," the Professor said. "Special permission."

"So, she won't get into trouble?" I said.

"No time for any more questions," the Professor replied.

Once the three of us were wearing our olive-green flight uniforms, we left the study and walked out onto the stone-paved landing area beyond the Professor's rooms. The sky was a very deep black that night and the stars seemed to be more luminous than usual. There was a cool wind at the summit of the great glass building. It blew on my face, bringing with it the recognizable odour of fuel from the spacecraft standing in front of us. As soon as I saw it, I was struck by its grey colours and its military markings. It was a Battle Ranger, with a cannon on its back, protruding from a glass bubble.

"This is my own vessel," the Professor said. "And it's equipped with the same jump drive technology as your father's was. This will give you extra speed. Meena's put in many hours flying it already."

I couldn't wait to climb on board. The vessel looked so sleek and lean and mean on the outside. I was sure that the interior would be impressive too. And it was. Illuminated by a low-level infrared light, the cockpit was as minimalist as it could possibly be. There was one monitor on the console, with a set of thumbnail icons, each containing symbols that pointed to their function. There were two seats set before the console, both with curved joysticks sticking upwards from the black carpeted floor. The pilot's stick had a red trigger button on the un-ribbed side of its curved handle.

"Sit in the co-pilot's seat," Meena said to me as she placed her olive-green battle helmet over her head, pulling out the tiny microphone, speaking into its soft tip with assurance and authority.

"Thunder Butt, you're in the gun turret," she added. "We'll call you if we need you. Just be ready. We don't know who's out there watching us tonight, or what. You know what to look for."

"I do," a voice crackled, followed by a muffled blast. Meena and I looked at each other with raised eyebrows. We both knew what that sound was, and we were both grateful not to be in the gun turret with him.

I placed the Arokah stone on the floor behind me, then climbed into my seat, strapping myself in, gazing through the three thin aluminium panes, one at each side, one at the front. The central window lit up with numbers and grids as Meena began her pre-flight checks, pushing various icons on her screen, ticking off the items on her list.

I gave Meena the approximate coordinates of where Dad and I had landed, then she fired up the engines. A bloodred light, which I took to be located on the tip of the caudal fin at the stern of our craft, began to rotate and flash in the darkness.

"Permission to take off," Meena said.

"Granted," the Professor replied.

The thrusters were barely audible as we rose straight up into the night sky, hovering above the launchpad for a few seconds, the tiny lights of the many parties flickering from the streets, rooftops and windows beneath. Then the Battle Ranger pivoted to the right in a smooth and almost casual movement, pointing out towards the gateway at the edge of the dome. In no time at all we were there, waiting to be cleared to leave the dome.

"Over to you, Thunder Butt," Meena said.

The voice of an android sentinel came through our headsets. "BR 102, please identify yourself."

"I am Farrer Glin, Ahketan of Xona," Thunder Butt replied, his voice at a lower register - manly, commanding, almost aloof. He was clearly using his ingenious device. Everyone knew Farrer Glin's voice. It was often heard in the news and this was as flawless an imitation as it could have been.

There was silence.

Meena looked at me, a frown on her face. We both knew what was happening. The gateway was being manned that night by android sentinels, which was both good and bad. It was good in that androids were incapable of having hunches or intuitions. It was bad in that they used the latest voice recognition technology, and Thunder Butt's impersonation was being scanned and scrutinised.

"What is the nature of your mission, Ahketan Glin?"

Meena uttered a sigh of relief.

"To examine and measure the hole in the upper crust of Xona's atmosphere," Thunder Butt replied, once again imitating the Ahketan's speech patterns with his homemade device.

More silence.

More scanning.

More scrutiny.

Then at last, "You are cleared to go. Use portal 4. Patching in the coordinates now. Be safe."

The comment was kind, but the voice was mechanical.

Meena took hold of the stick and directed us manually through the portal in the exterior of the dome and then we were through, heading up and out towards Xona.

At a suitable distance, far from our planet, Meena spoke again. "Weapons check," she said. "You go first, Thunder Butt."

There was a pause, then the sound of the gun pumping salvos into the darkness, the light from the laser cannons piercing the black space behind and both sides of us.

"Check!" Thunder Butt shouted.

Then Meena lowered her visor, looked through the illuminated crosshairs in the glass of the central window, and pressed the red trigger with her index finger. The front cannons activated, pouring two straight lines of brilliant tracer fire from the conical snout of the Battle Ranger, clearing a path through a clutch of rotating boulders which broke into a thousand tiny fragments.

"Check," Meena said.

Meena pressed another icon on the screen, with the symbol of a black hooded figure. "Activating stealth mode," she said. The light inside the cockpit diminished to the lowest level possible, and the thrusters became silent, even while still working. Thunder Butt, who could see the fuselage of the Ranger from where he was sitting, spoke into his microphone, his voice full of amazement. "Stealth mode activated!"

"Check," Meena said. "From here on, no one says a word, unless there's an emergency." Meena's voice was calm and professional. She looked and sounded cool. I wished I was six years older.

The Battle Ranger activated the jump drive and sped towards our destination, the hole in the crust of Xona's atmosphere. We all knew that time was running out and that the aperture was closing, resealing itself using the spores from the planet surface. Nothing could have prepared us, however, for what we found when we arrived there a few hours later, after the jump drive had been disengaged. The opening was half the size it had been less than a week ago, when my father and I had passed through it on the way to Xona, and I had passed through it on my way back. Another day even, and it would be too small, the upper crust an impenetrable membrane, as it had been before, for thousands of years.

I could tell, looking at Meena, that she was awestruck. She had only ever seen images on a screen. Now she was seeing it all herself, within her reach, close to the wingtips of the vessel she was flying, the ice crystal material of the crust, throbbing with a kind of teal colour.

I lowered my visor and switched to a microscopic lens. This is what I had wanted to do the first time I was here, examine the structure of the crystalized crust, undetectable to the naked eye. I was amazed but not surprised by what I saw. Millions of tiny hexagonal shapes, all wedged tightly together, in a system of perfect unity and economy, unbroken right up to the edges of the hole, where the exposed lines, once fractured, were now healing, reforming, and resealing before my very eyes, as if a hive-mind was directing and manipulating the pieces into an inevitable symmetry.

A heartbeat later, we were through, the wings of the Ranger just missing the hard matter, staring with wide eyes and open mouths at the great, grey, and pitted sphere that was Xona, splashed by the fading colours of trees and flowers, about to fade away in the dying sun.

I felt a knot forming in my stomach.

As we drew nearer to the surface, the knot tightened.

It was Thunder Butt who broke the silence. "After we returned to normal speed, I thought I saw something out there," he said.

"What is it?" Meena asked.

"I can't be sure, but I thought I saw something against the glow of the blue-green crystal as I looked out behind us. A kind of shimmering in the atmosphere. A strange vibration. It might have been nothing. Just my optics. But I'd like to make sure."

Meena reached towards a flame icon on the screen and pressed it. "Activating flares," she said.

A stream of bright white lights burst from the underbelly of the Ranger, racing back behind us towards the upper atmosphere. Meena turned the Ranger, swivelling round in a perfect 180.

"Can you see anything?" Thunder Butt asked. He was now facing towards the planet surface.

We both peered into the distance, using our visors to change from microscopic to telescopic lenses and back again. There was still some light from the sun, albeit disappearing, and the visibility was reasonable. Whatever Thunder Butt had seen, or thought he had seen, it was gone.

"I see nothing," I said.

"If there's anything out there," Meena added, "we can't see it, but it can now see us."

"Sorry," Thunder Butt said. "Must have been my imagination."

"Keep looking," Meena said, as she turned the Ranger back towards the flowers and trees on Xona.

Then we both saw it.

A square-shaped space had been opened, large enough for the Ranger to land. Just like it had when Dad and I had come here.

I thought for a second I was reliving the first trip in a dream. Then I realised, as the Ranger descended, this was not a dream at all.

We were in stealth mode, all but cloaked from view, but the Creeper had somehow detected our presence and made a space where before there had only been a tangled chaos of moving tentacles and tendrils.

When we touched down, I could see the weed withdrawing, heading away into the growing darkness. Or maybe down. Down into the rockface of the planet. Down into the caves and the caverns. Down into the core of our mysterious and intriguing sister planet.

"Deactivate cloaking device," Meena said.

The red lighting in the cockpit increased. Dim white lights appeared beneath the nose and the belly of the Ranger, illuminating the granite surface around the landing gear at the front and rear of the vessel. As the sun disappeared altogether, we sat in silence, staring out into the barren, rocky landscape, the shapes of mountains silhouetted against the low light of the stars and our own planet.

Then it started all over again.

A light.

A miniscule light.

Flashing from a shape rising above the surface.

Signalling.

Beckoning.

Short bursts.

Long bursts.

One colour.

Then another.

I pointed it to Meena, but she had already seen it.

"Thunder Butt and Khali, you're heading to the light. Take the stone tablet with you. And take the hover stretcher with you just in case…"

"In case of what?" I asked.

"Sorry, Khali," Meena said.

"In case of what?" I asked again.

Meena sighed. She placed her hand on my shoulder. "In case you need to bring back a body."

"What are you going to do, Meena?" Thunder Butt asked her.

"I'll stay here," Meena replied. "The Professor has asked me to gather some soil samples from the surface."

Meena switched off the engines and detached herself from the pilot's chair. "Suit up everyone," she said. "We're heading out."

16
My Father's Spacesuit

It took a few minutes for me to adjust to the spacesuit and my breathing apparatus. It had been a long time since I had put on a spacesuit – two years, ten days and nine hours, to be precise – and on several occasions Thunder Butt had to remind me to slow my breathing. "You don't want to make your visor all misty," he said. "Let alone run out of oxygen."

We had left Meena back at the Battle Ranger collecting samples, and were now proceeding towards the light. When we reached the cave, the entrance was as enormous as Dad had described it to me. It rose up above us like the vast, yawning mouth of a predator. Even the rocky summit of the cavern seemed to be shaped like the top of a creature's head, making it look as if the entrance was locked in the very act of devouring its prey. Had we not already had an idea of what lay within, we would almost certainly have paused and maybe even left the place unexplored. "We need to light our torches," Thunder Butt said.

He reached round to his back, where the folded hover stretcher was attached to a small backpack. He withdrew two torches and switched them on, handing one of them to me. Then he stepped behind me.

"I'm just checking the tablet's fastened properly," he said.

I could feel him tightening one of the straps.

"I still don't know how you manage to carry this thing," he said.

"One day you will," I replied.

Thunder Butt stood in front of me and checked that Meena was still patched into our comms. "We are at the entrance of the cavern, Meena," he said. "We are entering now."

"My thoughts are with you, Khali," she said. "Be careful both of you.""Thanks, Meena."

As we walked over the threshold, the lighting changed. No longer were we walking in the light of Kel. We were now making our way into a thick darkness, disrupted from time to time by the blinking light from somewhere in the distance ahead of us. Thunder Butt led, thrusting his torch this way and that as he followed what looked like a path along the edge of the right-hand wall of the cavern. Even in the low light, I could see tiny rivulets of water running down the rock next to me, falling like miniature mountain streams from somewhere above, across our path, and then down, down, down, into the chasmic darkness on my left-hand side.

"Stay close to the wall," he said. "There's quite a drop now."

Twenty-five steps later, we were faced by an opening in the rocks ahead, leading towards the light.

"I assume it's this way, Khali?"

I activated the infra-red setting on my visor. The opening to the tunnel was dark, except that a phosphorescent mark was on the wall just inside the entrance. It was the same squiggle that Dad used to write on official documents at the Space Academy.

His signature.

"It is."

I pointed to the letter Dad had drawn. "It's my father's marking," I said. "He's left us some signposts."

"Just as well," Thunder Butt said.

Before we entered the tunnel, Thunder Butt put his hand up to stop. "Meena, do you check?"

"Check!" she said. But I could tell there was a faintness in the message; it wouldn't be long before the signal was lost.

"We are deep in the cavern now," Thunder Butt said. "It may go silent very soon."

"Check," Meena replied. Then she added, "Keep an eye on your oxygen levels and use the backup supply if you need to."

"Check," Thunder Butt said.

We stepped into the tunnel and made our way down a long granite corridor. The damp ground was littered with small rocks, stones and pebbles. The slippery walls were covered in geometric patterns and hieroglyphs, like the strange symbols on my stone tablet.

After five minutes of trudging, synapses of memory began to flicker and flare. I was eight years old, sitting next to my father in our apartment, while he pulled up some photographs on the screen of his pad. The previous day, we had been to the hospital to see a neuro-therapist in a bright white coat. She had given me a scan to assess the condition of my brain. "I want to see if there have been any alterations in your whole brain neural activity," she said. It had been our routine, annual visit.

Dad had pointed to a set of images captured by the tiniest camera on our planet. It had penetrated the various areas of my brain, proceeding like a probe through trenches and pathways, exploring the dark areas that should have been ignited, the regions that should have been connected. At the end of it all, Dad had said that my brain was like a labyrinth. "I'm going to do everything within my power to light up the pathways that are dark and dormant," he had said, placing an arm around my shoulder.

As I walked down the dark tunnel of the cavern, following in Thunder Butt's footsteps, I raised my torch towards the ceiling, and then to my left and right along the walls, and finally down to my feet. *This labyrinth is my brain*, I thought. *I'm lighting up the pathways.*

Remembering my father's words brought me back with a start. The light ahead seemed to be growing larger. We were drawing nearer to the source of the light, or being drawn nearer, I wasn't sure which. And the nearer we came, the closer I was to finding out what had happened to Dad.

I felt the knot again in my stomach.

Anxiety.

Maybe stronger.

Fear.

I knew Dad was dead. I had gone through every possibility in my head, working out each scenario with a logic that was clinical. Dad couldn't be alive. There was no oxygen down here. He would have run out of air in no time at all. He would have lost consciousness as his breathing slowed to gasps. He would have suffocated. And we would find his body somewhere in the vicinity of the light source.

With a vacant stare.

A bloated face.

Just like in my dreams.

I had prepared myself for this in my room at the Beacon. But now, near to the discovery itself, I felt far from ready. This was my worst fear, seeing the suffering that my father had endured. Yet, it was also my greatest need. To find out what had happened. To know for sure that Dad had really died. To lay his body to rest. To experience at least some small comfort in the closing of his eyes and in saying farewell.

When the tunnel ran its course, I was diverted from my fears by the vision before us. An underwater lake, shimmering in a wash of light, stretched out before us at the bottom of a path that descended to its shore. It was enormous, surrounded on both sides by granite formations that resembled unformed pillars, like the imperfect shapes children make when they start to manipulate wet clay.

Thunder Butt followed the path around the sparkling water until we reached a flat and open space beyond. The light was strong now. Almost burning my eyes. I had to alter my visor to cope with its radiance. It seemed to be pouring from a source that I couldn't see, somewhere beyond the range of my vision. Dazzled as I was, I couldn't make it out.

We switched off our torches, which were now redundant, and fixed them in the loops in our back packs.

Just as we did that, the light began to shrink into a shape that looked like a sphere, no larger than the Battle Ranger.

"It's a gigantic orb," I shouted.

Thunder Butt nodded.

The sphere was now turning, its light refracting from tiny fissures whose pattern I recognised.

"Hexagons!"

My companion nodded again.

As the orb came to a halt, the tiny hexagons went dark, as if invisible blinds had been drawn over each one. Only a small part of the orb was emitting light now and it shone in one direction like a torch, towards the ground to the left of our vision, just a stone's throw away.

As I tried to see what it was illuminating, Thunder Butt, who was standing a few steps in front of me, turned and looked at me. I couldn't read the expression on his face. But when he reached out to lay a hand on my shoulder, I knew what it meant.

I walked out from his shadow.

There, jutting out from behind a cluster of heavy stones, were my father's white space boots, lying on one side in opposite directions. They were completely still. There was dried mud on the soles.

I felt myself beginning to freeze.

Pushing the dread down, I approached my father's body.

Then I saw him. On the ground, facing up towards the ceiling, and I knew he was gone.

Except, there was something not quite right.

He looked thinner. Far thinner. In fact, his spacesuit resembled a deflated balloon. It looked limp and empty.

It was unmistakable. There was no body inside the spacesuit. There was no bloated face behind the visor and there was no lifeless, vacant stare. The whole thing was completely confusing. The visor hadn't been removed and the suit had not been undone. It was as if my father's body had just disappeared, somehow passing through his suit and visor, from the inside out. But how could that be? There was no technology known to me that could do this. Maybe it was an illusion, a trick. Maybe it was another dream.

I reached out and touched the suit. It was tangible. Physical. Real. And it was his suit. The markings, the design, the identification numbers. Proof that this had belonged to my father.

"How can this be?" I asked, turning to Thunder Butt who was leaning over my shoulder, looking at the scene.

He shook his head, confused as I was.

I stood and looked at the orb. Its light was still trained on my father's spacesuit and I was caught in the same sun trap, along with Thunder Butt. The irony was not lost on me. Here I was, bathed in a bright light, and yet I was completely in the dark. What had happened to Dad? Was he wandering around the tunnels in his flimsy undergarments? If he was, how had he penetrated his suit without disturbing it? How was he still breathing? Wouldn't he be freezing cold and terrified in the cave?

I sensed a panic rising from my guts.

I couldn't stop it this time.

My mind, so used to working out even the most complicated puzzles, couldn't solve the most important puzzle of them all. The one I most wanted to master and complete.

And so, once again, I pictured the stone tablet. We became one. I was the stone, and the stone was me.

I was frozen in my father's puzzle, unable to move, but conscious - sentient, aware of my surroundings, at the same time no longer controlled or even affected by my emotions. Present. Observing. Thinking. No more anxiety. No more fear. No more panic. Just stasis. Serenity. A stable state of absorbing and being absorbed.

Absorbed!

That was when I understood.

Abs – orbed.

My body relaxed and my muscles became free again.

I looked at the orb, the light shining on my father's spacesuit, and I saw the beam begin to change, as if in response to my enlightenment. It seemed to me that it was no longer shining on my father's suit; rather, the suit was emitting and transmitting a light towards the orb. The direction had changed. The flow had reversed. The orb was no longer sending. It was receiving. And it was receiving from the place where my father's suit lay limp and empty on the stone-cold floor of the cave.

"Do you see it?" I asked Thunder Butt.

"The orb," he cried. "It's a tractor beam!"

The suit was rising into the air, floating in the white shaft flowing into the orb, moving towards the sphere, as if it was being sucked into the very heart of the light. The suit never changed its shape. It travelled in the same form as we had found it on the ground. Just as my mother was carried by Dad and me, and our friends, at her funeral. Until it reached the sphere, where it disappeared. Drawn into the burning light. Immersed. Transformed. Absorbed in the orb. No longer material, but invisible and intangible.

And then the direction of the light began to change again, sending not receiving, no longer trained on the place where my father's spacesuit had been, but moving from there towards me until it stopped, its ray causing me to raise a hand in front of my visor.

The light dimmed, as if understanding that my eyes were hurting. Its beam shrank into a line, targeting my chest.

"No!" Thunder Butt shouted.

"It's all right," I said. "Let it do what it needs to do!"

As Thunder Butt stepped aside, I felt the warmth in my heart as the light beam passed straight through me, from the heart of the sphere into the stone and Lagentum tablet.

The orb wanted the stone.

I thought I had been searching for the orb, but the orb had been searching for the stone tablet.

This was what the tablet had been for, all along.

I removed the tablet from my backpack and placed it on the floor of the cave. As the light from the orb began to flow into the tablet, I watched as the orb itself grew dimmer and dimmer.

"Wait!" I cried. I sensed the flow decelerating, then pausing. "I need to know…" I said. "We do not want to leave with all the power. We need to know that this isn't all the energy you have."

No sooner had I spoken than a thousand other brilliant orbs appeared in the walls and the roof of the great cavern, all around us, above us, among us, dismissing the darkness. Different sizes. Different colours. Like the lush hues of the flowers and the trees that sprung up each day from the creeping weeds that came out of the rocks of Xona.

As the orbs appeared, so did the sound of music. A chord. Extended. Harmonious. Notes that I recognized. Notes that I had never heard before. It felt like an invasion and recalibration of my senses. It was almost as if I could see the music and hear the light.

And then I knew. I knew that there was so much more than what the orb was giving to the stone, and what we would be taking to our home world, to bring a new and life-giving, lifesaving, resource to our planet.

"All right!" I shouted.

The orb resumed its transfer of energy into the stone, the light pouring and pouring until at last it was done, leaving the sphere empty, a cracked shell, a dull, matt, metallic black colour.

As the music began to fade, along with the light from the orbs, we took our torches and reignited them. I hauled the tablet onto my back and prepared to leave the hive of lights.

I looked again to where my father's suit had lain and felt a pang of sadness spread like a shadow across my heart. I had not found what I had expected. I still had so many questions. But I knew that at least part of my father had been absorbed in the light, even if it was just his spacesuit, and that this light was now in the tablet, and in a sense, in my heart, through which it had passed on its way to the stone.

I sighed and the mist from my breath covered my visor.

Thunder Butt saw it and, once again, placed his hand on my shoulder.

"It wasn't what you expected, was it?" he said.

I shook my head.

"Are you all right?"

"We need to get back to Meena," I said.

Thunder Butt turned away and we began to walk to the path around the lake. This time I led the way and we walked down the tunnel with the hieroglyphs and then along the edge of the cliff face, until we reached the mouth of the cavern.

After adjusting to the light, we checked our oxygen levels and activated our reserve supply.

Heading towards the Battle Ranger in the distance, I began to transmit. "Meena, we are coming back. Do you receive?"

No answer.

"Meena, do you receive?" I repeated.

"That's strange," Thunder Butt said. "It was working perfectly before. She should be receiving us ok now we're outside the cave."

The Time Keeper around my wrist began to grow warm. I shuddered. "Something's wrong," I said. "I can tell."

We accelerated and kept sending signals to Meena. No answer. The closer we came to the Battle Ranger, the more the Time Keeper burned on my wrist and the more alarmed I felt.

And then we saw it.

Right behind our own, another craft had landed. It was a much darker colour than ours, and it had been partly hidden by our vessel, partly hidden by the darkness.

Thunder Butt recognised it straightaway. "That's the vessel I saw at Rock Face's place. The one with the Pilot Droid sitting in the cockpit."

I could tell from his breathlessness that he was concerned.

"We've got company," he said.

17
Have a Medivac Ready

Moments later, we were confronted by our worst fears. We had approached the Battle Ranger from the side, treading as quietly as we could through the sand and stone, and I had noticed that the door to the cargo bay had been opened and the ramp lowered. Neither Thunder Butt nor I could see into the belly of the Ranger. It was pitch black. Even the low level infra-red lighting had been extinguished and we couldn't see anything. Except shadows. And then one shadow. The shape of a grown man. Or a woman. And something taller behind. Poking. Nudging. Pushing.

Thunder Butt lit his torch and raised it high. "Meena, is that you? What's going on? We're worried. You haven't been replying to our transmissions. Talk to us. Please!"

Just then we heard a yelp, and I winced. It was Meena's voice. Unmistakable. And she had just been hurt.

We rushed towards her.

"Stop! Do not move!"

The voice was cold and robotic, each word over enunciated.

"It's the pilot droid," Thunder Butt whispered. "The one I saw at Rock Face's place. It must have followed us here using a cloaking device."

"Where is it?" the droid demanded.

"Where is what?" Thunder Butt asked, adding, "Pointless pile of scrap metal!" I couldn't believe how rude he was. But then I remembered what he had said on our journey here, that droids are just machines, programmed to react to voices and words, not to insults or insinuations.

"The stone," the droid said.

"What stone?" Thunder Butt said. "Didn't your master teach you to be more specific? Use your words."

The pilot droid stepped forward, forcing Meena to go with it. As she came closer, we saw that her face was pale, her right shoulder drooping under the pressure of the black metallic hand clutching it. As soon as Thunder Butt saw that, his mood changed. Even the slightest tightening of the robot's grip would rip Meena's suit, and we both knew that Meena would be dead in thirty seconds if that happened. It was time to comply.

I looked at Thunder Butt. "I'm going to take off my backpack and remove the stone," I said.

He nodded.

Just then the droid reached with a spare hand to his chest and drew a gun from a metal holster encased in his gloss breastplate. He pointed it at the metal collar between Meena's torso and her head, where her neck would have been. She didn't move a muscle or say a word. She was being braver than I thought possible. Everything within me wanted to save her. One tragic death was quite enough for one day.

"It's here," I said, drawing the tablet from the pack.

The droid stepped away from Meena and stretched out the hand that had been attached like a claw to Meena's shoulder. She reached out and held her injured shoulder while the droid kept its gun trained on her. With its free hand, it beckoned to me.

"Give me the stone," it said.

I looked at Thunder Butt. I didn't want to let go of the tablet. It had a piece of my father, and a piece of me now too. It was the last connection I had to Dad. But I didn't want Meena to be hurt.

"Look at me," Thunder Butt said. "In a moment, you're going to give the droid the tablet. But I want you to do exactly what I say." He tilted his head to see if I'd understood. "Exactly," he reemphasised.

I nodded.

"Right," Thunder Butt said. "Chuck it to him."

The second he said it, I was back in my parent's kitchen, hurling my plate into the sink. I lifted the tablet and threw it towards the droid. It saw what was happening and gesticulated with its arms, reaching out with both to catch the stone as it travelled towards it.

The droid had reacted well, but it was caught off guard. The enormous weight of the tablet turned it into a weapon. Like a giant's sling shot, the stone hit it with enormous force in the chest, breaking its ink black breastplate, snapping joints and wires, disabling its weapon, causing the robot to teeter, fall back several steps, and threaten to fall.

If we thought it was all over, we were wrong. The droid was broken, but it was not finished. The machine recovered its balance, stood upright, stared momentarily at the broken breastplate hanging from its chest, then reached down towards the tablet on the ground. It tried to lift it, but the weight of the stone and the ruptures to its systems prevented it from lifting it any more than the distance between my wrist and my elbow.

Dropping the stone, the droid turned on me. It moved, first slowly, then accelerating. Thunder Butt, seeing what was happening, ran to intervene, but the droid stretched out its metal, skeletal arm and brushed him aside with one almost casual gesture, causing my friend to shoot through the air and land perilously close to a rock. There he lay stunned, gasping for breath, as the droid came for me.

I don't know what it was. Human instinct, or the energy from the spores, or a mixture of both, but I seemed to see the droid in slow motion, not in actual time. I stepped to one side as the machine attempted to crush me with its fist. It missed as I shifted, lurching forward, off balance, trying to stay upright. Swinging back and around, I grabbed hold of the droid, my arms around its fractured chest, and started to squeeze.

For the next thirty seconds, I became aware for the first time how powerful the spores were. In a normal fight, I would have been snapped like a stick and killed without any doubt or delay.

But I had Arokah on my side.

And I was strong.

Stronger than I had ever dreamed possible.

Stronger than any ordinary man or woman.

Stronger than a droid.

Instead of me snapping, it was the droid's frame that started to fold and collapse as I squeezed more tightly every second. The machine, computing that it was in danger, tried to wriggle, squirm, kick and chop, but to no avail. The more it struggled, the more I squeezed, and the more I squeezed, the more the sound of snapping increased.

As I sensed the droid dying, I lifted my right hand and thrust it around its neck and broke it in one quick jolt. The machine fell to the ground, limp and helpless, wires protruding from the fracture between its shoulders and head, sparks dancing here and there like fireflies.

I looked down. For once, perhaps because they weren't human, I was fascinated by its eyes. They were flickering. Fading. Moving from side to side as if confused, trying to calculate the loss of motor functions, analyse its error patterns. Intrigued by its own demise.

Thunder Butt shuffled to my side, panting. "You did it!" he said. "You are so strong, Khali!"

Just then, we both realised that we had forgotten our friend. Only when we stopped clapping each other did we see her, lying a little way from the debris, on her side, motionless.

"Meena!" I cried.

We ran to her and tried to make her respond. She didn't speak. She didn't make a sound.

Then we both saw it. A small hole in the side of her suit, round shaped, with burns in the fabric around its frayed edges. The droid's gun had gone off before trying to catch the tablet and a tracer bullet had pierced Meena's suit, appearing to pass through the right side of her chest, through her rib cage, and out the other side, leaving burn marks and flecks of blood.

"I must get her inside!" I cried.

I lifted Meena and carried her into the Battle Ranger, closing the doors of the cargo bay, laying her down on a bed, as Thunder Butt restored the lighting and checked the oxygen levels.

"We're good," Thunder Butt said.

I removed my visor and my spacesuit. Then I took off Meena's visor and carefully withdrew her arms from her sleeves and pulled down her suit, beneath the level of her shoulders, right down to her waist. There was blood all over both sides of her abdomen, seeping from the entrance and exit wounds. I started to apply pressure on the holes with my fingers, stemming the bleeding in both, at least for a while.

"Quick!" I shouted. "Find me the samples Meena took."

Thunder Butt hurried to the storage unit at the rear of the Ranger and started to press the release mechanisms in the glass cylinders in one of the freezer chests.

"Soil Sample 1," he cried. "Will that do?"

"Yes!"

He ran towards me, carrying a small tin, no larger than the one with my beeswax, and I took the finger of my right hand from Meena's wound, which started oozing dark red blood once again.

"Open it," I said.

Thunder Butt removed the cap and I plunged my finger, now wet with Meena's blood, into the sand and grit. When I pulled it out again, my finger was covered in dirt. Not only in dirt, but in the spores that poured from the planet, some of it returning to the dust of the surface when the weed retreated into the rocks at dusk.

"What are you doing?"

"I'm using the spores to heal her puncture wounds," I said.

"Will that save her?"

"I don't know. I can only see what happens on the outside. There may be damage to Meena's internal organs. I can't tell just by looking. We need to get her to a hospital and fast."

As I applied the sand to Meena's bullet holes, they started to close, and the bleeding stopped.

"That's only temporary," I said. "There's going to be internal bleeding, I'm sure."

Just then, Meena gasped, like someone gulping for air after drowning and being resuscitated.

"What happened?" she said with a groan.

"You've been shot," I said. "We need to get you to a hospital."

"Help me to the cockpit," she said.

"Are you sure?" Thunder Butt asked.

"I'm the only who can fly us home," she said. "Just keep me alive long enough to navigate through the opening and set the autopilot. There are some boosters in the med kit. If I lose consciousness, just inject me."

Thunder Butt rushed to the med kit in a locker behind the pilot's seat while I lifted and carried Meena to her place. "Here," he said, handing me the box. "I've still got my suit on. I'll just fetch the tablet."

The door hissed once, then twice. In no time, he was back, with the tablet hanging from his right hand.

"I don't believe it," he said. "Light as a feather!"

"I told you you'd be able to carry it," I said. "It's the energy from the orb. You've been changed by it."

"I'm an enhanced Thunder Butt," he cried, a broad grin on his face. But then he heard Meena groan again.

"Thunder Butt," she said. "You know what to do when we take off, with the droid and its vessel."

"I do."

"Let's get on with it," Meena said, her voice softer now. "No time for systems checks. Just this once, I'm going to ignore them. Don't tell the Professor, boys. It's our little secret."

"Our little secret," we both said.

The engines began while Thunder Butt removed his suit, climbing up into his gun turret, preparing the weapons, making ready to fulfil Meena's request. The Battle Ranger rose from the ground as Meena manipulated her controls. Every movement seemed to cause her pain. I, who sat next to her in the co-pilot's seat, looked on, helpless, anxious, wanting to freeze for my own sake, wanting to stay present and alert for Meena's.

"Now," she said, as the Ranger rose and tilted to the right.

The cameras at the rear of the vessel broadcast their images on both of our visors in the cockpit. We saw the droid. Re-energised by its backup power supply, it was pulling its immobilized body along the ground, clasping the soil and the stones with its lean metal fingers, trying to gain traction in an attempt to return to its jet-black runabout, now visible in the swatches of light from our Ranger's beams, moving like the patches of white on the Professor's blackboard back at school. Then Thunder Butt let loose a steady stream of tracer fire, first into the dredging droid, then into its stationery spacecraft. Both were cremated in the incineration that followed.

"It's done, Meena." Thunder Butt's voice came through the headphones in our olive helmets.

"Good work," she said.

Then we ascended, like the spores of Xona, up towards the dark crystal of the membrane, heading for the hole, hoping that there was still enough room for us to escape and return to our home world.

From time to time, Meena seemed to drift out of consciousness. I roused her by pushing her on two occasions. On one, I had to inject her in her thigh with the booster, which worked straight away.

As we drew near to the hole, Thunder Butt stepped down from his gun turret and joined us in the cockpit, setting up a third seat behind ours, looking ahead through the front window, searching, as we were, for the sign of the opening in the upper atmosphere.

When we saw it, we all three could see that it had shrunk even more while we had been on Xona.

"We were away a little too long," Meena said. "No one's fault. It was just how it was meant to be."

"What are our prospects?" Thunder Butt asked.

Meena gingerly pressed some icons on the screen on the console. "Not good," she said. "There's not enough room for us to pass through the hole. The wings will break."

"It's that small?" I asked.

"I'm afraid so."

"What are our options?" Thunder Butt asked.

"I can think of only one," she answered.

She pressed some more icons.

"Never been done before … Very dangerous."

Meena slumped forward, her body limp, her head leaning sideways towards me.

"Meena!" I cried, shaking her hand.

No response.

I withdrew another booster.

"How many of those has she had?" Thunder Butt asked.

"Two now."

"She can't have a third," he said.

"I know."

Meena came around with a jolt and looked again at the screen. "How long was I out?" she asked.

"Four seconds," I said.

She nodded and then pressed an icon on the screen that showed the Ranger with folded wings, as if it had come straight off the assembly line, packed tight, ready to be shipped.

She accelerated towards the hole, then shut down the engines, and touched a button on the screen. Through both side windows, we saw and heard the wings retract into the body of the Ranger, tucking themselves into the fuselage, turning us into a slimmer version of what we'd been before. Then we started to glide towards the hole, Meena staring through the windows, then through the navigation grid in her visor.

No one spoke.

We could all see what was happening and we all knew that our chances were as slim as our vessel. If anyone could do it, Meena could.

She manoeuvred the vessel to within a Ranger's length of the opening, then we all instinctively braced for impact. But the impact never came. Not even the sound of the Ranger scraping the shrinking hole. We passed through it without a scratch or a sound, gliding through it as quietly as an arrow loosed by a master bowman.

It was the finest flying I had ever seen.

On the far side of the hole, we cheered, Thunder Butt patting Meena gently on her arms, telling her that she was truly amazing, which was one of the biggest understatements of my life. She, meanwhile, ignored our compliments, restoring the wings to their regulation position, turning on the engines and restoring the vessel to full power.

When Thunder Butt and I had calmed down, Meena reached forward to the screen, pushed the autopilot icon and then spoke, her voice almost inaudible now. "Whatever happens, we'll get home. The coordinates and the jump drive are all pre-set. We're heading for the Professor's landing pad. You might need to tell him to have a medivac ready for me."

"We will," I said.

Meena seemed to be on the edge of sleep now, slipping in and out of her awareness of what was happening, trying with an almost superhuman effort to stay awake to ensure that we made it home.

Thunder Butt disappeared into his glass bubble, keeping an eye out for any more of Reikhl's droids.

An hour from the sentinels, and another display of Thunder Butt's unique skill for impersonation, Meena's eyes opened and she looked at me, her head leaning right, her face towards me.

She turned off her comms so that Thunder Butt couldn't hear.

"If I don't … don't … make it …" she stuttered. "Bury me with my … auburn hair," she said, before gasping, falling silent, and then drifting away like a leaf on a stream.

18
To the Lighthouse

The automatic pilot behaved without any glitches, taking us back to the top of the Space Academy Headquarters as the darkness began to fade and splashes of orange light heralded the dawn of a new day. All the way back, I sat next to Meena, holding her limp hand, talking to her, encouraging her, telling her everything was going to be just fine. I never stopped whispering. During my mother's last days, when she was unconscious, Dad had said, "Mum's hearing will be the last thing to go. You can keep talking to her. She will hear you even if the rest of her seems to be somewhere else." One time, as if to confirm Dad's point, Mum had squeezed my hand when I told her that I loved her, that I would always love her, until the day I too made the journey into what Dad used to call "the Great Beyond". I waited for Meena to squeeze my hand. But she never did. Not once.

Touching down on the Professor's landing zone, I saw the medivac. Its red lights were flashing.

The Professor took my arm and told me to look at him before he too stepped onto the medivac. "Put on your qark costume, Khali. Go back to the Beacon. Pack and get ready. I'll pick you up at midnight."

"Where are we going?"

"To the Temple," he said. "It'll be your new home." Then the Professor pointed to the tablet under my arm. "We should take that too. You can place it in the table when you arrive," he said.

I nodded and handed over the Arokah Stone to Thunder Butt, who lifted it effortlessly, carrying it into the medivac, where he sat next to Meena. She was lying on a stretcher, her eyes closed, her face pale, her olive-green helmet lying by her side, her auburn hair flowing from her head, just as I had arranged it, seconds before we landed.

"Be careful with the stone," I said to the Professor. "It contains the energy of one of Arokah's orbs and I don't yet know what it does, or what it's capable of doing."

"I'll wait until you're with us at the Temple," he said.

Then I looked at the medivac. I could make out two people, about the same age as Meena, already attending to her injuries.

"Members of the Class of 24," the Professor said, understanding the problem I had with facial recognition. "They are the best at what they do. Meena is in safe hands."

"Will she make it?" I asked.

The Professor didn't answer. He simply raised his wispy, grey eyebrows and frowned. Then he walked to the medivac, clambered into the belly of the vessel, strapped himself in, and gave an order to the two pilots, who I figured were also members of the Class of 24.

I watched as the medivac rose into the night, then swung away in the direction of the edge of the dome. I was alone as I walked back to the Professor's quarters where, after stroking his aging qark, I dressed in my costume and headed down again to the lobby, passing the fountain with the big fish, then walking out into the cool air, down the avenue of trees, back to the Beacon.

That day was also part of the National Holiday, a rest and recovery day after all the parties the night before, so the concourses and pavements were empty apart from a few stragglers struggling to return to their quarters, moving clumsily along paths and roads, teetering and tottering in their fancy-dress costumes, stumbling and groping in the half light, desperate to reach their beds, as I now was, but for very different reasons.

When I returned to my room, I removed my outfit, dressed in casual clothes and spent the morning packing. When everything was in bags, I stored them out of sight in the wardrobe, then popped into the empty canteen for some lunch. I hadn't eaten any breakfast, consumed by my worry for Meena. Now I felt hungry and eating a creamy toffle-waffle for brunch boosted my energy levels before I returned to my quarters. For several hours after that, I sat with Shin, not saying a word, conscious of Thunder Butt's warning that the walls in my room might have ears.

Late afternoon, as the sun began to go down again, I had a shower and then flopped down on the bed, utterly exhausted from the all-night mission, drained by the emotions I had felt while seeing Meena suffering. I had had my fill of loss and grief. Meena had become a true friend. She had put her career on the line for me. She had put her *life* on the line to help me in the search for my father. I owed her. I owed her big time. But I also needed her. Her friendship had become a high wall, keeping the floodtides of loneliness away from my heart. "Loneliness," my father once said after Mum died, "is not having anyone to share your secrets with." I loved that Meena had shared her secrets with me, and me with her. I would never share them with anyone else. If there's one thing about us Rhuboid kids, we are loyal. And we don't just say it. We live it. One hundred per cent.

As Shin nestled under my arm, burying its snuffling nose into my chest, sleep came without a struggle. It was a deep and restless sleep in which I dreamed without stopping until the time I woke. To begin with, I was back in the cave, searching for my father, finding his spacesuit. Then I was standing in the Temple, staring at the tablet almost in a trance-like state, looking intensely at the Lagentum plate with the shapes and the letters. As I looked, a message began to form. I heard the words on the plate. They were in my father's voice. He said, "Your heart is flesh, but mine is stone."

It was the final dream sequence that disrupted my sleep the most. I turned on my bed towards the cupboard opposite me. Light began to pour out of the lattices. Not a warm orange or white light. A red light. A threatening, dangerous light. And somewhere within the recesses of the wardrobe, something moving, moaning as it shifted one way or another, sniffing at the tops of my bags, searching for something, uttering a deep throated growl as it failed to find whatever it was it was looking for.

In my nightmare, I was sweating with the terror, paralysed in my bed, unable to move this way or that, incapable of opening my mouth, of uttering a cry for help.

The cupboard door opened.

Out of the shadows, a form emerged.

Two slanted eyes.

Large canine teeth.

Powerful jaws.

Long muzzle.

Pointed, upright ears.

Black ridged back.

Dark-tipped tail, hanging straight down.

Swollen, dripping teats, dangling from the yellow-white fur of its underbelly.

It was a predator.

A beast from the forests of Carlon.

Like one of the night hunters of the Great Plains.

It was low to the ground, its head growing larger the nearer it came, its forepaws reaching up towards the end of my bed.

I tried to scream but I was frozen.

The creature climbed onto my feet, then up my legs, over my belly, onto my heaving chest.

Crushing.

Suffocating.

Its teeth were over my face, saliva drooling over my nose, its throat like a dark cavern into nothingness.

As it prepared to strike, I felt the weight of one of its back paws on my left wrist, bearing down, squeezing tightly, burying its claws into my flesh, burning me with the pain. Then up, into my left arm, which was now shaking violently, uncontrollably.

Then a voice.

"Where is it?" the creature hissed.

I couldn't answer.

Then some light. Not much. Half-light.

Breaking out of sleep.

Escaping the nightmare.

The predator had disappeared.

It was Matron, tugging at my left arm, then holding it hard, like a piece of metal in a vice. My Time Keeper was throbbing, buzzing, scolding my wrist. Shin was cowering on my legs, eyes jet black, nails digging into the bedsheets. Frightened.

"Where is it?" Matron repeated. "The stone tablet. The puzzle your father gave you. Where is it, boy?"

No darlink, I noticed. Just "boy".

"I … I … Haven't got it."

"I can see that. Who's taken it?"

"No … no one."

"Liar!" She pulled me from the bed and stood me upright before her face. Her eyes were fierce.

"Let go of me!" I shouted. "You're hurting me." I took hold of her arms and thrust them away from me, shrugging off her armlock as if she was no stronger than Shin.

Matron looked surprised at my strength. Then something seemed to register in her thinking as her shock morphed into determination. She reached behind her back and drew a weapon from her belt. "Come with me!" she said, more a growl than a voice.

I stepped back towards the bed where Shin had hidden. I had seen the same gun in the hands of the droid on Xona, and I'd witnessed its lethal power in Meena's seeping wounds.

"Bring your qark," Matron said.

Shin's eyes were begging me not to take it, but the gun was pointing at my back and I had no choice.

"Where are we going?" I asked.

"If you say another word, I'll use this," Matron replied.

Then out of the cubicle, into the darkened, quiet corridor, down past the canteen, out through the kitchens, to a yard behind, filled with skips and bins, some reeking of rotting food and damp cardboard.

There was no one in sight.

It must have been nearly midnight.

The rain was falling from the opened skylights in the dome, gently at first, then louder, soaking Shin's hair, turning it into a wet, forlorn and bedraggled companion.

"In there!" Matron was pointing to a black, metal elevator shaft that ran up the far side of the Beacon, right to the summit, where the lighthouse was flashing on and off. It was the highest point in the city, even higher than the launch pad at the top of the headquarters of the Space Academy.

What was she doing?

I opened the door and climbed into the elevator with Shin, Matron's gun digging into my back, pushing me deeper into the darkness.

No words.

Just the sound of the lift mechanism.

Up and up.

The rain coming down on my face, on Shin's face.

When we reached the top, Matron made me open the door. Then we were out. Amid the antennae and masts, the ducts and funnels, white and wet with the pelting rain, illuminated and then darkened as the monumental bulb of the lighthouse turned this way and that.

"There!"

Matron was pointing to a low wall that ran along the end of the roof, beyond which I knew there was a long drop to the ground at the foot of the Beacon. No one could survive a fall like that.

When my toes were touching the wall, she made me stop. I could see the rain cascading onto the pavement below. I imagined I was a solitary raindrop, descending from the roof, splashing into the stone, crashing into the slab amid the dispersed and wet chaos of my fall.

"Where is the tablet?" she asked again.

"At this precise moment, I do not know." That was literally true. Therefore, not a lie.

"Don't play games with me, boy."

"I'm not." Then I added, "You're the one playing games. You're pretending to be our Matron, all nice and kind. You're working for Reikhl. You're a liar and a cheat!"

The smack that came as I said the word "cheat" stung worse than a bee. Matron had struck me with the butt of her weapon. I toppled backwards, my body lurching towards the abyss behind me. I could feel my lip beginning to swell, blood on my tongue, along with the taste of the rain, as I tottered at the edge of the precipice.

"I'm not done with you yet," Matron shouted, pulling me back. "I will ask you one more time. Where is the tablet?"

"I don't know."

Matron's face turned to thunder. She pointed the gun at me and shouted, "Put the qark down."

I placed Shin on the ground, trying to keep it out of a puddle spreading in all directions at my feet.

Matron stepped away from me and pointed her weapon at me, then at Shin, who looked up, hair matted and tangled by the wind and the rain, eyes now filled with tears in the rain.

"Where is it?" The light from the revolving bulb fled from her as she spoke, throwing her face into darkness. I had been counting. When the light moved, we were being consigned to the shadows for exactly two seconds. I had two seconds to make my move. I had the strength of Arokah. If I could just reach the woman, I could pick her up as if she weighed no more than her gun, and hurl her over the edge of the wall, into the deep and deathly darkness where she belonged.

But I was not alone.

Even before I made my move, I saw a shape behind her, moving out of the background of my vision, into the foreground. As the white light returned, I saw the glint of his crystal epaulettes.

It was the Guardian.

And he was wrestling the gun from Matron's hand.

As the weapon fell to the floor, they began to fight. I had never seen such moves before. Matron, who I had not thought of as agile, was springing from one foot to another in almost robotic precision, thrusting and chopping with her hands. The Guardian was even nimbler, parrying and thrusting, fending off one blow, taking another one on his arm which he had stretched out to protect himself from the full force of the strike, aimed at his throat.

For what seemed like ages, Matron shimmied and ran, this way and that, trying to gain the upper hand.

Just then, everything changed. The Guardian's golden medallion was swinging in front of his chest when the bulb of the lighthouse swivelled round again, casting a bright ray of light in his direction. The light caught the metal, reflecting from the pendant, blinding Matron as she attempted to kick the Guardian. Startled, she stumbled, fumbling and groping, trying to regain her balance and momentum.

But she was too late.

There were five crystals that hung in front of the Guardian's forehead, each one the size of a blade. There were two that were slightly bent on each side and a longer straight one in the middle. He grabbed hold of the central crystal and thrust it once, cleanly and precisely, into Matron's body. She reeled, fell backwards, landing on her back.

She groaned.

Gasped for breath.

Desperate to inhale.

Unable.

The Guardian stood over her. He took the crystal blade, wiped it, then returned it in front of his forehead, where it seemed to slide into some invisible dock. He drew up the sleeve of his long-hooded cloak, revealing a livid wound that ran the length of his lower arm. Matron had injured him in the fight, and he was bleeding.

Taking one of the bended crystals, the Guardian placed its curved end in short, mechanical movements over the open wound, dabbing it from one end to the other. It sealed the tear, stemmed the flow of blood, leaving a large scar.

Yet another scar.

Another predator.

Shin crawled into my arms, fur sodden, eyes white. White as the light of the Beacon.

I watched from the shadows as Matron's face began to go purple. Her eyes stared up at the Guardian, wide, terrified, unable to resist the unseen hands that were already reaching into her, pulling her life force from her chest, wrenching it out and up into the night sky.

It was only then that I noticed the Time Keeper. As Matron died, it became cold again.

"It was her!" I cried. "It was Matron who made it burn me. It was warning me. Or trying to."

The Guardian turned to me and smiled.

"And you were trying to protect me when you came to my room and had an argument with Matron," I added.

"Not quite," he said. "You left your Time Keeper at school that day, so that misled me into thinking you were still in your classroom. I didn't realise you were hiding in your cupboard while I was looking through your things, trying to see if your dad had left me a message. It was Meena who later told me that you had been there."

"But I thought you were the shadow man," I said.

Then I understood. The shadow had never been the Guardian, as I had first thought. It had been Reikhl, who had managed somehow, no doubt aided by Matron, to gain access to the Beacon to try and terrorise me and rob the stone. All along, Matron had been a spy working for a man who wanted the Arokah for his own ends. And all along, the Guardian had been watching her, and watching over me.

"Thank you," I said, as the rain soaked my face.

"You should thank your father," he said. "He foresaw all of this. Whether it was the dreams that he was having, or just his brilliant mind, I'll never know. But he saw that you'd be in danger and asked me to protect you."

"So, you knew my dad?"

"I did. I used to fly with him on missions to Xona. Just him and me. In the Doxana. It was he who gave me the samples to use for the Hall of Spores, knowing that they would benefit Rhuboid students like yourself, even if the spores could not cure you."

Then the Guardian frowned. "And it was some of these spores that Reikhl has somehow managed to steal to use for his own ends, to rejuvenate his diseased flesh, to prolong his days, to give him time to rob Xona of its life in order to save his own."

I nodded.

"You will have heard about me," he said. "By another name, the secret name your father gave me, Danguari."

Everything was beginning to make sense now.

I had always thought his name was odd.

Not anymore.

It was an anagram.

Guardian!

As we walked away, heading towards the Guardian's Ranger that I now saw on the landing pad nearby, I stepped over Matron's dead body. As I did, I caught her dead eye.

"Goodbye, darlink," I muttered.

19
The Birth of the Arokai

Two weeks later, I was there when Meena woke from her coma-induced state to tell her what had happened after she navigated our Battle Ranger through the opening with an ingenuity now legendary in the Class of 24. I told her that Matron had been working for Rock Face. I shared how the Guardian had been watching over us, and how I had discovered that the Time Keeper was a warning system for me and a tracking system for him. None of this turned out to be new to Meena, nor to Thunder Butt, who had suspected Matron from the start, which is why he kept goading her in the canteen.

"It was the Guardian who assigned me to be your mentor," Meena said, her tone weary. "He asked me to be your watcher too."

"You did a good job," I said.

The only thing that was news to Meena was the fight at the lighthouse, on top of the Beacon Tower. "The Guardian must have known you were in trouble from the tracking device on the Time Keeper," she said.

"He rescued me," I said. "And Shin."

Meena smiled. Then she asked, "How's Thunder Butt?"

Just then, Thunder Butt appeared, a balloon on a string in one hand, a large box of sweets, already opened, in the other.

"Hello Meena," he said, accompanied by the munching of a chocolate. "Are you feeling all right?"

"I'll be fine," she said. Then she turned her head from side to side, observing her surroundings. She glanced through the window and saw the lush trees and flowers of the grounds outside.

"Are we in the Temple of Xona?" she asked.

"We are," I said. "The Professor brought you here after you were wounded. This is part of a hospital we are all building. He's moved all of us to the Temple – you, me, Thunder Butt, and the others."

"The others?"

"The Arokai," Thunder Butt said.

Seeing Meena's confusion, I stepped in. "It's the Professor's new name for the Class of 24, the Guardians."

"And the tablet?"

"It's called the Arokah Stone now," Thunder Butt interjected, "On account of the fact that the Arokah energy was absorbed in the tablet when Khali and I were in the cave."

Meena's expression changed, as if she was remembering something. "I'm sorry about your father," she said.

I said nothing.

"What happened?" she asked.

Thunder Butt took up the story, telling Meena about the journey from the time the transmissions stopped, down the tunnel in the cave, to the great lake, and onto the orb that was filled with the Arokah energy. He described my father's spacesuit and how the orb drew it into the light until it had disappeared altogether, then how the beam of light had changed direction, moving from the orb to the tablet, disappearing into the Stone.

"Have you placed the Arokah Stone in the Temple?" Meena asked, her face weary from the effort.

"Not yet," I said. "We were waiting for you to recover."

"Thanks," Meena said, shifting her position.

"Here," said Thunder Butt, relinquishing the balloon and the chocolates, pulling her pillow upwards.

"And what happened to you, Meena?" I asked.

Meena answered with a grave and laboured voice. "After you had gone into the cavern, I was collecting spores for the Professor when I heard something behind me, beyond our vessel. When I turned to see what it was, a dark grey Ranger decloaked and landed."

"The one I saw when I was spying on Rock Face," Thunder Butt said, his voice excited.

"I knew I was in trouble. The Guardian can't fly a spacecraft, so I realised straight away that it wasn't good. I was on my own. You guys were in the cave and I was isolated, an easy target."

Meena moved again before continuing, easing the pressure on the wound in her right side.

"The battle droid came down the ramp holding a weapon and demanded that I revealed where the Stone was. I said I didn't have it. He didn't believe me, so I told him to search our Battle Ranger. He made me go inside with him and search the vessel at gunpoint."

With that, Thunder Butt's bottom squeaked. It was a tiny sound, but we both heard it. And a second later, we both smelt it.

"Were you scared?" he asked.

"It doesn't really help being scared," Meena said. "You've got to stay calm, Thunder Butt. And try and hold things together."

"Especially your butt cheeks," I added.

Meena managed a smile. "I was pleased to see you when you returned," she said, "although I was also concerned that the droid would take the Stone, and worse still, harm you."

"You stood up for us," I said.

"You'd have both done the same for me."

Just then the door slid open, and the Professor walked in, a broad smile on his face.

"Glad to see you doing better, Meena," he said.

Meena nodded.

"I have some news for you."

Meena looked up at him.

"Your graduation day has been set in one month and fifteen days. By then you should be fully recovered. There will be a ceremony at the Space Academy for all the students, where you will receive your pilot's scroll, and then we will have a ... little get together ... here, at the Temple, where we will show our appreciation for what you and these two have done."

The Professor then turned to me.

"And you will place the Arokah Stone in the table, Khali," he said. "It will be a most singular honour and a most significant turning point in the history of our planet."

"Thank you," I said.

"Don't thank me yet," he said. "There's more. The Guardian and I have made a decision."

Just as he said that, the door opened again, and the Guardian walked in. He looked even more cool in the light of the side ward. I had only ever seen him in the half light of my room in the Beacon, and then of course under the night sky at the top of the Beacon Tower. Now I could see every line, every furrow, every scar on his rugged, stubbled face. And the hovering crystals! In the light, they seemed to shimmer and chime like the orbs of Xona.

In the bright light, the Guardian was also wearing small dark glasses, with round lenses and a gold frame, underneath a hood which partly covered his dark long hair. When he smiled, one of his lower front teeth was as golden as the medallion hanging from his thick neck.

"Meena," the Guardian said, walking to the bed and holding her hand. "I am relieved to see you looking better. You must take your time. There's no hurry. I want you to rest as long as you need."

Meena's eyes became teary as he spoke.

The Guardian, sensing this, turned to me. "And Khali, you have done admirably well, as have you, Loois, or should I call you Thunder Butt? Even Shin has contributed. You make a formidable team."

The Professor nodded.

Then the Guardian reached out his hand and took my left wrist. "Let me adjust the settings on this," he said, removing the golden Time Keeper and pressing one of the four round dials on the facia. "I will make sure that it doesn't burn you in the future."

Then he handed it back to me and said, "I'm sorry. I had to guess. I knew your Rhuba would make you extra sensitive, but I didn't know how much. This should now be better."

The watch wrapped itself around my wrist.

We were about to leave Meena to rest, when she waved her hand to stop us. "What about Reikhl?" she asked.

Thunder Butt answered. "I have been on another one of my spy missions. It's not looking good. Rock Face is livid. Mad at us. Mad at the Professor. Mad at the Guardian. He's planning something, I can tell. He's been in communication with the Timba Corporation. I think he's planning to pay them to build something. I don't know quite what yet."

"He's causing trouble," the Professor added. "He's stirred up his supporters in Parliament. He wants to blast holes in the membrane and rob Xona of its energy."

"Will they use your weapon, Professor?" I asked.

"To begin with, until they realise it doesn't work. But it will only be a matter of time before they adjust it. Then, I'm afraid, there will be an all-out plundering of Xona's resources."

"Does Reikhl ... sorry, Rock Face ... know about the Arokah Stone?" Meena asked.

"Not yet," the Guardian answered. "All he knows is that his droid failed. He doesn't know how or why, and he doesn't know about this place, or that the Stone is now here."

"Not yet, anyway," the Professor added.

"Not yet," the Guardian agreed.

"Which is why," the Professor continued, "the Arokai are fortifying this Temple, with higher impregnable walls, an invisible shield, and concealed defence armaments around the perimeter. From now on, this will be called the Temple of Arokah."

You could have heard a surgical needle drop.

"And from now on," the Professor concluded, "the Class of 24 will be known as the Arokai and will be devoted to two causes: education and intervention. You will continue receiving an education here within the Temple, where all of you will live. And you will do everything you can to intervene and disrupt the attempts to exploit the Arokah energy source."

"Everyone will have a role in this," the Guardian said. "Especially you, Khali."

Every eye seemed to be upon me, as if I had been lit up by a hundred infrared scopes.

"You have a very special relationship with the Arokah Stone," the Guardian continued. "Your father, my late friend, poured out his heart and soul into making that tablet for you. There is more of him in that stone than we will ever know. You are the only one who truly understands its mysteries, Khali. So, you must look after it."

"For that reason," the Professor said, taking over, "We have all voted that you shall be called the Doyen of Arokah. You will ensure that the power of the tablet is used wisely and well."

The Guardian reached into his long, flowing coat and drew out an object made of gold. It was a medallion, a smaller version of the one that he himself wore, only with a picture of my father's tablet engraved upon it, not a lighthouse. It was attached to a strap.

The Guardian placed it over my shoulders, so that the pendant was hanging in front of my chest.

"In Meena's presence," he said in a solemn voice, "we appoint you the Doyen of Arokah."

There was a brief silence.

"What's a doyen?" Thunder Butt asked.

The two men laughed.

"It means the most respected, distinguished, experienced person in a particular field or subject," the Professor said, once he had stopped chuckling. "Khali qualifies as that, when applied to the Stone. The Stone is his father's heart, frozen in time. It is also a puzzle, which he alone managed to solve. So, I'd say that makes him the Doyen."

Everyone in the room nodded, except me.

"One more thing," the Guardian said, producing a small, golden box from the folds of his coat. Placing it in my hand, he said, "This is for you."

I opened the lid and there, beneath the glass of the box within the box, was a solitary bee, buzzing and twitching, its six legs and six wings trembling as I held it in my hand.

"Is it?" I gasped.

"It is," the Guardian whispered.

Tears began to form in my eyes.

"I'm sure you thought your father's bees were gone forever," the Guardian said. "But they're all safe and they're all here in the grounds of the Temple. They are waiting for you to look after them."

"And we are waiting for them to produce honey for us," Thunder Butt interjected.

Everyone laughed.

"Thank you," I said, my voice faltering.

"Let's be on our way," the Professor interrupted. "We need to let Meena rest and recover."

As we made our way out of the room, Meena beckoned for me to stay behind.

"Don't be long," the Professor said. "She's very tired."

I nodded as they left.

"What is it?" I asked.

"You won't believe it," she said.

"Won't believe what?"

"Just come over here, Khali."

I moved to the edge of the bed.

"Hold this," Meena said, leaning forward, taking my hand and placing it on her auburn hair. "Now pull it!"

"No way," I said. "It'll come off."

"Do as I say," she insisted.

After several more attempts to resist, I agreed.

I pulled.

"Harder than that!"

"Don't forget I have Arokah's strength, Meena. I could end up pulling your head off, like that droid on Xona."

"Just do it," she said.

I pulled again.

Then it dawned on me. Meena's auburn hair was still in my grasp. The wig was not moving.

"Is this a new, enhanced wig?" I asked.

"No," Meena laughed. "And you can let go now."

I stepped back, looking at Meena's hair. There was no sign of any slippage.

"It looks … almost … well … real!"

Meena laughed again.

"It's the spores," she said.

"What do you mean?"

"I'm cured," she cried, tears forming in her eyes. "The spores have cured me. My hair has been restored. This is real hair, not a wig, Khali. It's amazing hair, too. It just falls into place, the way I like it, the way I'm thinking at the time. And it's so … so full of life. I just can't get over it!"

I began to laugh too.

Until Meena grew serious and started to pout.

"What's the matter?" I asked.

"It's nothing, really."

"No, go on. Tell me."

"You promise you won't laugh."

"I promise."

"Well, okay then. Up until now, I've never had to brush, cut, style, shampoo, spray, shave or anything while I was wearing a wig. I've been saving a fortune! Now I'm going to have to buy all this stuff. I'm going to be broke all the time."

I laughed as I stepped towards the door. "Don't worry," I said. "I've got plenty. You can borrow mine."

"Thanks, Khali," she said. "You're a good friend."

And with that I left, smiling as I strolled down the empty corridor of the brand-new hospital, delighted that at last I had a friend who, like me, was passionate about hair.

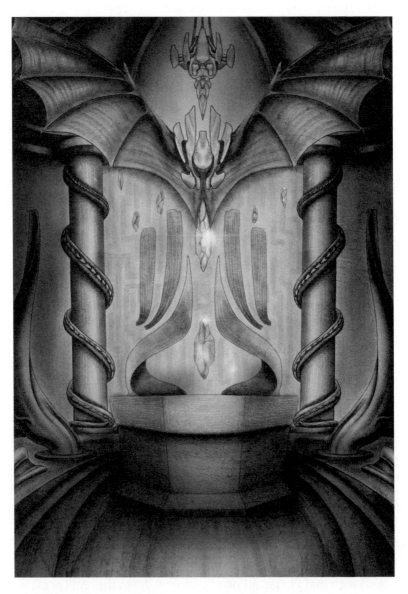

We passed through some ornate doors into a great chamber,
with what looked like a stone table on a dais at the far end,
under a canopy of dragons' wings carved in gold.

20
The End of the Beginning

One month and fifteen days later, when Meena had fully recovered, we gathered with every student from the Beacon, including the Class of 24, in the main square at the school. This would be the last time the 24 members of the Arokai would ever be seen in public with the rest of the students from the Academy. From now on, we would be living and working at the Temple, preparing for the troubled times ahead as the storm clouds gathered over Kel. But that's another story, for another time.

All of us cheered when Meena received her pilot's scroll. She looked so pleased and happy under the blazing sun, with her bright white wings now sewn into both the epaulettes of her olive-green uniform. She was hailed in the introductory remarks as the most outstanding pilot in her year, even perhaps in a generation. The applause that followed the Admiral of the Fleet's speech was loud and heartfelt, especially from Thunder Butt and me, who knew first-hand the price she had paid.

There she stood, her auburn hair protruding from the back of her cap – real hair, rejuvenated by the spores of Arokah. I was so pleased that she was my mentor and friend.

I couldn't have been prouder.

As we watched the ceremony, Thunder Butt nudged me. He was standing to my right in a uniform that seemed one size too small for him. His cheeks were reddening under the blazing sun as his waist battled with the fabric of his uniform, threatening to stretch and even tear it.

"I know what he's up to," Thunder Butt whispered.

I said nothing.

"Rock Face."

"Not now, Thunder Butt."

"Yes, now, Khali. He's approached the Timba Corporation to help him mine the membrane. He's planning to use the crystals to develop warbirds with jump drive engines."

I shuddered as I remembered the message on my father's tablet.

"What do they look like?" I whispered back.

"Birds of prey," he answered. "Rock Face is designing them like his helmet, to resemble Night Ravens. He wants them to look terrifying, and he wants them to be invincible."

I shuddered again.

The Admiral dismissed the parade and Thunder Butt and I resolved to continue the conversation another time. For now, the priority was to celebrate Meena's achievements, which we did by raising her on our shoulders and carrying her off to a lunch in the Professor's rooms.

Every member of the Class of 24 was invited, and every one of us enjoyed the snacks and treats the Professor provided, and we all enjoyed meeting Splink, his aging qark.

Throughout the celebrations, I noticed that Demorah was sitting alone and had a faraway look, even during the meal. When she left early, I followed her out into the classroom.

"Demorah," I called. "Are you all right?"

She turned, a surprised look on her face. It seemed to me that she was not expecting anyone to think of stopping her from leaving. It also seemed to me that the power of Arokah was improving my perception of other peoples' faces. If this carried on, Shin would become redundant.

"I'm tired," Demorah answered.

I didn't believe her.

"Do you want to talk about it?" I asked.

"About what?"

"About what's really bothering you."

"Look Khali, I don't mean to be rude. It's just that I don't make friends and I don't need friends. I prefer my own company. At least then, if I feel let down, I only have myself to blame."

"Why would you want to blame yourself?" I asked.

"I blame myself for everything. For the fact that my mother abandoned me. For the fact that Meena, not me, was up there today achieving what she's achieved. Everything. I'm just not good enough."

"Have you always felt like this?" I asked.

"Maybe, deep down, but it's only been the last few months I've felt it like I do now."

"Why now?"

"You really want to know?"

"I wouldn't be asking if I didn't."

Meena paused, then sighed, then spoke. "I discovered that my mother had been alive all these years, that she had never contacted me while I've been at the Beacon, and now I've learned that she's dead. So, she's left me a second time and I'm really, really angry about it."

"I'm so sorry."

"It's not your fault, Khali."

"It's not yours either," I replied.

Just then, I heard some movement behind me. The Professor and the Guardian were standing at the door to the study, talking with serious faces to a small, bespectacled boy just inside the Professor's room. It seemed that they were about to leave the celebrations.

"Anyway," Demorah said. "I've got to dash."

"I'll see you tonight at the dinner, won't I?" I asked.

Demorah hurried away without answering.

That night, in the Temple, the Arokai gathered with the Professor and the Guardian for a spectacular feast in the gilded dining hall. I wore my golden medallion in public for the first time.

I sat next to the small boy in the large spectacles that I had seen at lunchtime in the Professor's rooms. It turned out that his nickname was "the Boffin", on account of his extraordinary inventions, which now had been even more greatly enhanced by his nearness to the Arokah energy. This had given him even more advanced knowledge and had led both the Professor and the Guardian to ask him to build something important, something big, something all the Arokai would need in the future.

"What is it?" I asked as I finished my last course, a silver plate of candy bars and beans.

The Boffin tapped his nose. "Need to know basis," was all he said, but then he had said little during the meal. Like me, he had Rhuba, and like me, he didn't find it easy interacting with strangers.

"Well," I said. "I need to know."

"All in good time," the Boffin replied, looking dead ahead, avoiding all eye contact with me. "All in good time."

When the dinner ended, the Professor gave a speech and called us all to raise our glasses to Meena, which everyone did with a great roar of admiration. He then shared that he had appointed me to be the Doyen of Arokah, and Thunder Butt to the role of Spymaster. He said that there would be roles for all the Arokai, not just the three he had mentioned, and that each of us would have a vital part to play.

"The darkness is getting darker and thicker," he concluded. "But you are all of you carriers of the light of Arokah. And together, we shall not let the darkness rob Xona of its power, nor use the power of Arokah for its own ends. We will do all we can to resist, and we will prevail."

We all shouted and clapped when he finished.

After the feast, the Professor told us to leave the hall and head into the Temple. Everyone followed me in a silent procession as I carried the Arokah Stone to the table on the dais. Placing it carefully over the groove, I slid it into place. As we all looked on, the Lagentum plate glowed in the light of the guttering candles and its letters seem to dance across the shapes.

It was the Professor who spoke as I stepped away.

"Let me remind you," he said, turning towards the table. "The energy we call Arokah is neither good nor evil. In the right hands, its power can be used to heal. In the wrong hands, its power can be used to harm. It is our task to make sure it is used for good. That will be our choice, a choice that will become harder when night falls. We must do everything we can to prevent this Stone from getting into the wrong hands, and we must do everything we can to make sure Xona is treated with the utmost respect and dignity."

He paused and looked away from the Stone towards us. "We want the best of both worlds and the best for both worlds."

We all repeated the mantra, in unison, and the words echoed around the chamber as we left in silence.

Later that night, I returned to the Stone, carrying Shin under my arm. I had spent the afternoon downloading the contents of the Time Keeper onto my communications pad, watching as the software programme, called Narrator 004, transformed my memories of the last week into a story - *this* story - just as the Guardian had promised. I marvelled at the way it transformed the fragments of my experiences into an orderly chronicle. Even though some of the words were not my own, the voice was, and I was pleased with it.

Now I stood in the sanctuary of the Temple, looking down at the beautiful floor. The entire space had been tessellated in recurring patterns, each shape a perfectly designed hexagon, each hexagon a different colour, just like the ones I had seen in the cave my father had discovered. None of these hexagons overlapped, nor were there any gaps at all between them. The floor was a masterpiece, like the rest of the Temple.

As I gazed at the tessellation, a wave of sadness broke upon me like an unexpected wave. I missed my father with an ache that I will never be able to put into words. For the first time, I felt angry that he had chosen to leave me and pursue the light in the cave. I knew in my head that his reasons were sound, but in my heart, I felt so hurt that he had relegated me, his only son, to second place beneath his need to discover Xona's secrets.

I looked up at the table. "Why?" I screamed. "Why Dad? Why did you abandon me?"

As the tears came, I became aware of two people, one either side of me, close to my arms. It was Meena and Thunder Butt, who had followed me and watched me from the shadows. They sat with me as I cried into my qark, which I was holding in front of me, soaking its hair.

After what seemed like a long time, the sobbing stopped, and my body ceased its terrible juddering.

I was staring with my friends at the Stone.

It had begun to glow.

The shapes and letters had started to shift.

Before I had time to rub my eyes, a message formed.

"I am with you always, my son."

Then a familiar greeting.

"Me to you. You to me. Forever."

Without thinking, I spoke the same words.

Then, in the heart of the sanctuary, the Lagentum plate began to change colour.

From slate to purple.

Purple to orange.

Orange to gold.

Before it finally became a shimmering, tranquil teal.

The colour of my father's eyes.

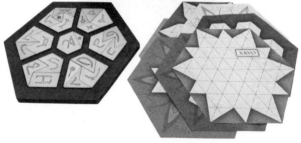

The Chronicles of Arokah

Khali and the Orb of Xona is a gripping and original Sci Fi fantasy that explores the mysterious origins of Arokah. It follows the journey of Khali, a young orphan who has a condition known on his planet as Rhuba. He is an autistic boy in an autism-friendly world. The book is aimed at 9-year-olds and above, and has been highly praised by readers and experts who work in the area of Autism.

The *Arokah puzzle* represents one of nature's best kept secrets: a unique and fascinating set of shapes that encompasses the inherent beauty of nature to create the ultimate multi-puzzle challenge.

The appeal of Arokah is its symmetrical, patterned nature with differing levels for all abilities, endless combinations of pieces and solutions, all contained within a tactile and portable puzzle. People with autism often have a highly logical brain that can understand, find and manipulate patterns with ease. As the Arokah puzzle could be of great interest to the autistic community, it is intended to evaluate its potential usefulness both as an aid to relieve stress and as a clinical diagnostic tool for autism.

Acknowledgements

We are indebted to some very special people who read this first Arokah story in an early draft and offered invaluable advice.

Some of these advisors are experts in science fiction and children's stories, others in specialist areas from teaching and parenting children on the autistic spectrum to those knowledgeable about other medical conditions also important to the story.

We are very grateful to Charlotte Anderson, Richard Cole, Jamie English, Lynda Evans, Saul Kitchen, Michelle Lemar, Nicola Shaughnessy, Rachel Wilkinson, Claire Worsham and others. Any failings in this first story are not due to these wonderful people, but to us!

We are also indebted to members of our own families for their input and support. We couldn't have done any of this without the love of spouses, children, other family members and friends.

Finally, we want to thank Malcolm Down and Sarah Grace for believing in us and in this project.